DARK CHASE

Seth Sjostrom

*wolfprint*Media

 **wolfprint**Media

wolfprint, LLC
P.O. Box 801 Camas, WA, 98607

This book is a work of fiction. Names, characters, places, and incidents are products of the author's imagination or are used fictitiously. Any resemblance to actual events or locales or persons living or dead is entirely coincidental.

Copyright ©2020 by Seth Sjostrom

All rights reserved, including the right to reproduce this book or any portion of the book in any form whatsoever.

For information, contact wolfprintMedia, LLC.

Trade Paperback KDP
ISBN-13: **978-1-7349376-6-4**

1. Ryder Chase (Fictitious character)-Fiction. 2. Paranormal-FBI-Supernatural-Thriller- Fiction. 3. Dark Chase Series-Fiction I. Title.

First wolfprintMedia edition 2020

wolfprintMedia is a trademark of wolfprint, LLC.

For information regarding bulk purchases, please contact wolfprintMedia, LLC at wolfprint@hotmail.com.

United States of America

Acknowledgments

Nick, for your dear friendship as well as your fine-tuned sixth-sense in the field.

Michele, for being an original instigator in the paranormal.

Matt, for your endless enthusiasm which always brought levity to the darkest of corners of investigations.

Hayden, from my partner in-training to my second in command. There is nothing we don't seem to have fun doing together.

Kathi, keeping me honest and on the right path, even when exploring the dark and unknown.

My family in North Dakota (and beyond), none more fruit giving than the late Marion Powell teaching me faith, fruit of hard work and respect for farmers and small towns like the charming Hope.

For Hayden

DARK CHASE

ONE

A chorus of cornstalks rattled in the wind amidst the swirls of dust. There always seemed to be a breeze at this end of the field, with it, smells that were inconsistent with any of the other thousands of acres surrounding it. In the path of the warm wind was the Helberg house. Long since abandoned, the old farmhouse stood out against the encroaching field of corn, conspicuously planted in a wide swath avoiding the structure. No one in Hope liked to go near the place, even the farmer who leased the land.

Hank Sandquist was no different. Stopping well short of the rotted fence and weed-infested lawn in front of the house, he let his dog sniff along the ground. Hank studied the field as he did every day. The early August drought was playing havoc on the corn. Instead of even rows of consistent stalks, the field looked like it was planted on rolling hills instead of the slate flat ground he knew it to be. Then again, maybe it was the Helberg House. No matter how cheap the lease, he didn't blame the farmer for not planting anything near that godforsaken place. It wasn't an accident that he turned back on his walk each day at this edge of the field.

Turning away from the cornrows, bobbing in the warm breeze, he patted his leg to indicate it was time for he and Tuffy to head home. Not hearing the jingle of the collar or seeing the scruffy dog prance up to his side as he usually did, Hank quickly scanned between the rows for the Jack Russell Terrier. As he heard the excited bark to his left, his heart sank. Normally well-behaved, Tuffy was confronted with his greatest weakness - a rabbit sniffing along the overgrown weeds had shown himself, and Tuffy had sprung into chase mode. To Hank's dismay, the whole fracas was leading straight to the sagging porch of the Helberg House.

"Tuffy!" Hank called desperately, breaking into a reluctant jog. "Tuffy!"

The terrier was locked on and defiant of any other stimulus than the rabbit. In a full sprint, the exuberant dog raced after the cotton ball. At the last second, the rabbit lunged, disappearing into a sliver-thin gap between the rotted steps and the dirt. The hole too small for the dog. He refused to be stymied and began digging furiously in the dirt to get to the rabbit.

Out of breath, Hank paused to gather Tuffy. One eye on the house, one on his dog, he grabbed at Tuffy's collar. Suddenly, the terrier yelped and jumped back. Running and curling behind his master, he stared at the house. "Serves you right, Tuffy. Now, let's get out of here," Sandquist scolded his dog.

Relieved to be leaving this nasty place behind, Sandquist turned toward the street. Just as he passed the now-defunct gate, a call sent the hair on his neck straight in the air. A very faint, desperate "Help!"

Closing his eyes, Hank stopped in his tracks. His mind oscillated between shaking off the call as the wind and turning back to investigate. Before he could make up his mind, a second, more pleading call traveled through the air. "Pleeeaase!"

This time, the voice was distinct and clear. Hank was sure the voice was that of a child. Tuffy cocked his head, looking up at his master. The dog seemed intent on continuing home. Hank took a step away. He was sure he heard the child. In one determined action, he turned and strode steadily to the house. His foolish concerns canceled by the need of a child, he stormed to the porch. Picking his way through the perilous derelict front steps, he tried the handle on the door. Swinging open easily, he called out, "Hello?"

Unsure, he thought he heard a muffled cry from the interior of the house. Swiping away cobwebs, Hank carefully made his way down the hall towards the back of the house. The floorboards felt soft, urging him to test his steps as he went. Again, he called out, unclear if he was receiving any feedback. His blood pulsed, but out of adrenaline, not fear. The former Vietnam Vet was determined to face any challenge he had to in order to save the child. Finding his way to what was once the kitchen, he heard a thump from the pantry closet.

Moving swiftly, he grabbed at the pantry door and turned the knob. To his surprise, the knob turned back against his grip, fighting him. In a mighty pull, Sandquist freed the door, ready to strike what nefarious person was toying with him and the child. As the door opened, Hank washed in a flood of terror and internal pain. Sitting cross-legged on the floor in front of him was his daughter, a wicked grin crossing her pale, marred face. Hank clutched at his chest, crumbling to the floor. He wanted to run. He wanted to stare at his daughter. He could do neither, as his racing heart suddenly froze. It beat its final beat as he stared face down at the dusty floor. His last breath blew up a cloud of dust around him. A giggle shattered the overwhelming silence. A giggle from his daughter that had died thirty years ago, falling out of an oak tree, not far from this very farm.

Special Agent Jeffers settled into the conference room. Leaning back in his chair, he sipped from a mug of coffee that had an image of a bullet ripping through screened on to the ceramic surface. "What's on tap?"

"Strange case out of North Dakota," Agent Danica Sohn said ominously. She relished her new role in hosting the assignment briefings. It was traditionally the duty of the senior agent, in this case, Jeffers. A month ago, he suggested she take over the job to gain additional experience. It meant she had to come in early and prepare to roll files out to the team, a trade-off as the department recognized her as more of a leader.

"Oh?" Jeffers yawned.

"Better than the last case, I hope," Agent Dunlap, the rookie of the team, snorted. "Wasting the FBI's time on some stupid bomb threat - just a kid trying to get out of his midterm."

"This one is real...mostly..." Sohn replied.

"Mostly?" Jeffers asked.

"Real people. Real dead," Sohn answered. "Six of them in the last three weeks."

"How?"

"Heart attacks, it appears."

Dunlap shrugged, '"People die of heart attacks all the time."

"Six in a town of about 150. Some were in their late teens."

"Sounds more like a CDC thing," Jeffers said.

"They called *us*."

"So, what are they thinking? A rave? A bunch of kids getting ahold of some bad 'X'? You mentioned teens," the team leader suggested.

"Middle age women in a farm town hopped up on ecstasy?"

"Probably not a rave," Jeffers conceded, "Power lines?"

"That's cancer cells," Sohn shook her head.

"Insecticide from the farms?" Dunlap offered.

"They checked. None found that would be lethal or affect the cardiovascular system."

Then Sohn paused, "There was one commonality, but you're not going to like it."

"What?"

"The townspeople all claim the victims had had a run-in at a particular house."

Jeffers raised an eyebrow, "And?"

"They say it's haunted and that the victims were all actually scared to death."

"What? A haunted house. You can't be serious," Jeffers exclaimed. "I'm not taking on a ridiculous case like this, forget it!"

"Chief says it's ours," Sohn claimed emphatically. Wrinkling her nose, she added, "You're not going to like this, either. You know that professor at the college that the local news interviewed a few weeks back…"

Jeffers' face reddened, "That kook yammering about ghosts? What about him?"

"Chief said he's on the case with us."

The lead agent blew up, slamming his fist on the table, "Oh, no. I'm not taking some worthless, crazy case, and I'm not babysitting a whack job. Tell Witt to give it to Haskins and Jensen, sounds like a good case for them."

Sohn shrunk a bit at her superior's reaction. "I think the chief was pretty adamant. It's *our* case."

"I don't care. No!" Jeffers reiterated, "I don't want the stinking case, and I sure as heck am not taking the ghost dork."

Just then, the door swung wide. Chief Witt stood in the doorway, trailed by another man. Dunlap, who had been rolling in laughter at the exchange between his fellow agents, suddenly snapped to attention. "Special Agent Jeffers, Agent Sohn, this is…" Chief Witt began.

A thin man in a poorly fitting suit pushed forward and held out his hand eagerly, "Professor Ghost Dork."

Witt pursed his lips and pressed in a stern tone, "Dr. Ryder Chase. He is an expert in parapsychology and is a national authority on cryptozoology."

"With all due respect…" Devon Jeffers pleaded.

"Agent Jeffers, there is no discussion. I expect you to welcome the professor and his team on this assignment. Show him the respect as though he is a fellow agent."

"Yessir," the agent muttered.

"Oh, there is one more thing," Director Witt nearly winced at laying more on the senior agent, "Dr. Chase is lead. You are there for security and to assist the local authority making any arrests as necessary."

The agent choked, "They're what?"

"Special Agent Jeffers, my team and I are excited to be taking on this case with you. Our role is attempting to identify any logical explanations for things and isolate those for which we cannot find a plausible explanation for," Chase tried to console the FBI agent who was glowering at his superior.

Jeffers looked doubtful, "And how exactly do you do that?"

"We explore the stories, try and recreate what they experience, and through a series of experiments determine if there is a tangible, organic source for the reports," Ryder Chase explained.

"No candles, séance...little splash of holy water?" Jeffers scoffed.

Dr. Chase seemed undeterred by the agent's reaction, "No. Just pure science, not unlike one of your investigations. Some of our witnesses can be a little tougher to coax into talking..."

"You mean ghosts," the senior special agent looked incredulous. He shot a desperate look to the bureau chief. Witt gave a slight head shake.

"Mostly, it is a lot of surveillance, history and interviewing of real, live people," Chase assured.

"Great. When do we leave?" the agent resigned.

"Soon as you can pack and get to the airport," Witt replied.

After a brief pause, almost waiting for someone to declare it was all a big joke, Jeffers slid his chair out. Surveying his team, his superior, and scarcely offering a glance at Ryder Chase, the agent left airing a sigh of disgust.

TWO

The arrival in Hope was unceremonious. The agents pulled in ahead of the professor's team, parking outside of what appeared to be the police department and town hall. With one major street, the location was easy to find, but left the newcomers quite noticeable.

The lead agent climbed out of the SUV and made a beeline for Chase's vehicle. Putting his hand on the sill of the open driver's window, Jeffers effectively blocked the professor. "Look, I don't care what Witt says. We are controlling this investigation. If you guys need to poke around or do whatever it is you do, you need to clear it through me, otherwise, stay out of the way," Jeffers commanded. "Now, we need to be as low key as possible so that we don't stir up a frenzy with these folks. This case is complicated enough without a big to do. Let me do the talking and follow my lead, got it?"

Dr. Chase nodded, "Fine by me, Agent Jeffers."

When Jeffers released his hand from the car door, the professor hopped out. Joined by his two team members, he followed the federal agents into the Mayor's office. The moment they entered, they were greeted by a young woman. Leaping out from behind her desk, she studied the group. Ruling out the two men in suits and their female companion, she locked on the other three men. Mentally knocking off the one with the somewhat disheveled appearance, she narrowed her selection down to two. Focusing on the tall man in front, she asked, "Dr. Chase?"

The professor nodded, "I'm Ryder Chase.

"We've been waiting for you!" the woman squealed. "Come on, follow me. They're in the community room."

Leading the six travelers down the hall, she opened a set of double doors revealing a room packed with people. Folding chairs set in neat little rows were overflowing with bodies, behind the rows of chairs, the walls stacked with more people. In front, six chairs sat empty on a little stage. As they entered, a hundred heads turned and followed them down the aisle.

Agent Jeffers was beside himself. A man squished into a suit shuffled up to them. "It's a pleasure to have you in our little town. I'm Jan Stenner, the Mayor."

"Mr. Mayor, I think we're all set!" a man called as he adjusted a microphone stand at the end of the middle aisle.

"Great! Let's get started," Mayor Stenner said. Turning to his guests, "As you might imagine, the town has a lot of questions, I hope you don't mind."

"Well, actually…" Jeffers began.

"Not at all," Chase said, leading his team up to the stage.

The three FBI agents looked at one another, still in shock over the impromptu town meeting. Jeffers sighed in disgust. This was precisely what he didn't want. Agents Dunlap and Sohn struggled to stifle little giggles at the situation and their superior's beet red complexion. "Perhaps we'll let Dr. Chase and his team handle the questions," Sohn suggested in a low whisper.

Fearing losing total control over the situation, Jeffers stepped in, "No, we'll join them, just in case there are any *real* questions concerning the case."

The six arranged in their seats, looked out at an expectant crowd. Mayor Stenner walked out to the middle of the stage and addressed the townspeople. "As you all know, there have been very sad and unfortunate events over these last few weeks. These folks here have flown in from D.C. to help us figure out what is going on and prevent any further harm to our friends and neighbors."

"If you would be so kind as to introduce yourselves?" Mayor Stenner asked as he turned to the panel.

The three agents tight-lipped, Dr. Chase sat up in his seat, "Sure. I'm…I'm Dr. Ryder Chase. I am a parapsychologist out of the University of Virginia School of Medicine. These are my colleagues, Wally Smyth and Don Tannen. Wally?"

The stout man next to the professor squirmed in his seat, "I'm in charge of the equipment our team uses."

"Don't be so humble. He's also a forensic scientist and a darn good one. He recently came to the University of Virginia on loan from the state crime lab," Chase added.

"By loan, he means state budget cuts," Wally admitted to laughs from the crowd.

Raising a hand in the air, the young Asian man next to Wally announced, "I'm Don Tannen. I am the second investigator and medic of the team."

After a long silence, Agent Dunlap spoke up, ignoring Jeffers' slight knee kick as he did, "I'm Agent Dunlap with the FBI. These are my colleagues Special Agent Jeffers and Agent Sohn. Glad to be here to help your town."

"Alright, let's get right to the questions," Mayor Stenner declared.

Without hesitation, an older woman came up to the microphone. After an excruciating squeal emanating from the speakers as she adjusted the mic stand, she asked, "This question is mainly for Dr. Chase. Do you think ghosts can kill people?"

Jeffers coughed at the question, finding the entire ordeal absurd.

Dr. Chase smiled and calmly replied, "No, ma'am, at least not directly. I have investigated numerous cases and studied thousands more. I find it highly unlikely that a ghost or other entity can inflict such direct harm as to kill anyone. They struggle to gather enough energy to emit a whisper, or a tap, or for those in my field, the ultimate in showing themselves as a visible apparition. Now, there are cases of people being shoved, or scratched or having their hair pulled. So, it's possible with that contact, people can be hurt. I would attest even in those cases, it would most likely be by accident."

Tannen and Smyth both nodded their agreement while the trio of FBI agents just stared in astonishment at the professor's earnest response.

Clearing her throat into the microphone, the woman pressed, "But what about without contact, Dr. Chase?"

"Well, I suppose that is what we are here to find out. According to the files..." Chase started but was quickly cut off by Jeffers.

"This is an on-going federal investigation; therefore, the details of the case and files cannot be discussed."

"That's all fine and good, Mr. Agent, but Hope is a small town. We already all know what happened," the woman declared.

"If you all know what happened, then I guess case closed. We can go home," Jeffers retorted.

Mayor Stenner stepped in, "What Agent…" the mayor stopped and looked over at the lead agent.

"Jeffers. Special Agent Jeffers."

"What *Special* Agent Jeffers is saying is that they must follow all normal protocols to do their job," the mayor concluded.

A man in well-worn overalls replaced the woman at the microphone. He bent down to where the last woman adjusted it, "Hello. I was wondering if you find something, what you can do about it."

"Well, if it is supernatural, there are a host of possible ways to expel it. Sometimes just speaking to it, letting it know it isn't wanted. Perhaps a holy cleansing…" Dr. Chase answered, "And if it turns out to not be paranormal, we have Special Agent Jeffers and his team."

"And we do pretty much the same thing. We talk to the bad guys and let them know they aren't wanted. They pretty much just hop in the backseat for us," Jeffers quipped.

"We have to speak more sternly, of course," Agent Dunlap added, putting levity to Jeffers sarcasm. The room erupted into laughter, including Dr. Chase.

"How do you know if a place is haunted?" another question came.

"That really is the tough part. We go into an investigation trying to *disprove* a haunting. We try to find logical answers to the claims. When we can't, well, that's the exciting part," Dr. Chase replied.

"Ideally, we capture either an image or a sound. We use a variety of video and audio recorders and other equipment to document what we find," Wally Smyth answered.

A young boy scurried up to the microphone, "Can anyone come help you?"

In unison, the entire panel cried, "No!"

Dr. Chase and Agent Jeffers looked at one another. "Finally, something we agree on!" Chase smiled.

Not nearly soon enough for Agent Jeffers, the town meeting was adjourned. The panel, mainly Professor Chase and team, answered a dozen more questions, most of them about paranormal research in general. Agent Jeffers immediately found the Steele County Sheriff, "After this circus, we need to make sure no one gets any big ideas and poking their nose out at the site in question."

"I can run patrols out there," Sheriff Ira Biggs scratched his head and replaced his hat, "But I dare say most of the town won't go near the place."

"It's the other side of 'most' we need to contend with," Jeffers said matter-of-factly.

"Yes, sir," the Sheriff said and dispatched one of his deputies.

The crowd dispersed, the six investigators gathered alone in the town meeting room. "So much for discrete," Jeffers cursed in disgust.

"Don't look at me. Doesn't make our job any easier, either," Chase admitted.

Jeffers looked sour, "No, I suppose not. We're losing daylight, might as well give this place a look."

THREE

The short drive to the Helberg house revealed a lovely town- the image of Americana. Children played in yards along the quiet streets. The people the caravan passed waved friendly greetings. As the van and the SUV cleared the last house on the main road, most of the horizon erupted in a sea of corn and soy plants. In the distance, a combine kicked up a dust cloud spinning and twisting into a farmland tornado.

Lonely farmhouses occasionally challenged the scene, most flanked by large grain elevators towering over the homes. In front of one of the houses, a stand stood in front of the driveway. A man lounged beside it; a straw hat pulled over his eyes.

"Dude!" Agent Dunlap cried in alarm, "Stop!"

Jeffers pulled the SUV to a quick halt on the side of the road. The van load of paranormal investigators slammed on their brakes and pulled alongside, narrowly missing the lead vehicle.

"What is it?" Jeffers asked, readying himself to spring out of the truck.

"Sign says 'Cold Iced Tea'. I forgot to grab something to drink from town. It sounds like we might be out here for a while!" the young agent leaped out of his seat. Looking back in the cab, he called, "Want one?"

Jeffers shook his head in disgust. To his further dismay, Agent Sohn unbuckled her seat belt as well.

Shrugging at the senior agent, she smiled, "Closest neighbor. Might have some insight. Besides, tea sounds good."

The paranormal team met the agents at the little stand. A hand-painted sign listed sweet corn, sunflowers, and vegetables in addition to Iced Tea. Big letters scrawled around the word 'Fresh' in the center of the board. Off to the side, a homemade placard added honey, herbs, and fresh fruit to the offerings. A sampling of the goods displayed in a variety of boxes and baskets, stacked around the booth. On the stand sat several jugs of brown liquid in different hues.

Behind the stand, in a chair leaned against a fence post, a man in overalls sat motionless, a wide brim straw hat shoved tight over his face. Wally looked at the farmer suspiciously, "Is he dead? Should we poke him?"

Don Tannen grabbed corn stalk and began leaning over the stand, stabbing the shoot towards the sleeping man.

Agent Sohn knocked the stalk out of his hands and glared, "What is wrong with you?"

The two paranormal investigators looked at each other and shrugged.

"Sorry, they don't get to talk to real, live people very often," Chase quipped.

Agent Dunlap was waiting at the bar of the stand, drumming his fingers against the rough wood. "Doesn't seem like such a bad idea."

"Nobody needs to poke anybody, I hear you," a voice from under the hat declared. Shoving his hat up, he cleared his throat. He sat silent for a moment taking in the motley crew. "What can I do for you?"

"Let's see…I'll have the bramble tea. What's in it?" Agent Dunlap replied excitedly.

"Little this, little that," the farmer said, "Our newest blend. Tasty though, give you a little zip."

"Zip, huh? Seems like a zip kind of day," Dunlap nodded.

"I'll have some of that stuff, too," Wally added.

"Straight up for me," Chase said.

"I'll have plain as well," Agent Sohn placed her order.

"You're those FBI folks, are you?"

Agent Jeffers sauntered up behind the group, "Doesn't take much time to for word to spread around here, does it?"

The farmer looked up at the tall agent and offered a sinister grin, "The corn told me."

Jeffers rolled his eyes behind his dark glasses, "You got anything other than tea? Can't stand the stuff."

The farmer paused, staring at the agent for a long moment. "Just the tea. I can fetch some water for you."

"Bottled?"

"Sweet North Dakota water- from the tap."

"Never mind," Jeffers mumbled.

As the farmer began pouring the beverages, Chase leaned against the counter. "What do you know of the Helberg house?"

The farmer pulled his finger off the tap that was filling one of the cups of iced tea. "Enough."

"What do you think of the place?"

"As much as anyone else, I suppose. Don't reckon I envy you all for having to go in there."

Chase looked at him, "You wouldn't go in there? Why?"

"Same reason I wouldn't jump into a pit of snakes. It's evil."

"What makes it evil?" Tannen asked, a hint of nervousness in his curiosity.

"It's why you're here, right? People die in there. With not another soul around, at least no living soul, drop dead just by going in there."

"You can't really believe that," Jeffers scoffed.

The farmer stared at the agent, his mouth agape. "I believe it. Don't even like being close to the place."

"What do you suppose makes it evil?" Professor Chase asked.

"Helberg," the farmer said emphatically, "He was a mean man. No one liked him. He didn't like anyone. Least not toward the end."

"Toward the end?" Danica asked.

The farmer grumbled, "He wasn't always that way. Used to be a decent fellow. When his wife and daughter died back about twenty-some years ago, he just snapped. Guess anyone of us might have given how hard it must have been on him. Still, hard man to tolerate after that."

"There you go, professor. A grumpy ghost," Jeffers needled.

"I say just burn the place down," the farmer recommended, his tone icy serious.

"Thank you for your time," Danica Sohn thanked the old man.

"Man, this is good iced tea!" Dunlap declared, raising his cup in the air as he climbed back into the black SUV.

Three miles of corn later, the investigation team arrived at the Helberg house. Dunlap pulled the FBI issue SUV off the road and alongside the dilapidated fence, crunching over dry weeds that spilled over from the unkempt yard. The vanload of paranormal researchers backed into what they perceived to have once been the driveway. It, too, had been overrun with vegetation.

For a few moments, all six investigators assembled in front of the old farmhouse. Staring up at the partially sunken porch, the paint flecked from years of neglect. The whole structure seemed sad, lonely, forlorn. Suddenly, a cool breeze cut through the warm afternoon, bringing with it a stale air. A loose shutter rattled violently against an exterior wall.

"So, this is it..." Wally called to no one.

Dunlap stared at the farmhouse, "Man, just what you'd picture a haunted house to be."

For several moments, the investigation team stared at the house.

Breaking the quiet observation, Jeffers grumbled, "Let's get this going."

"Why don't we do a walkthrough, get our bearings, and then we'll set up," Chase suggested. Turning to his tech manager, "Grab the EMF, might as well get baseline readings."

Wally opened the back of the van and produced two handheld instruments. Handing one to Don Tannen, he pushed the button on his and watched the L.E.D.s flash denoting the unit was operational. Seeing the rookie FBI agent cast a curious glance, he responded, "KII meter. Senses changes in electromagnetic frequency. This model is pretty simple, but the L.E.D.s makes it easy to see quick hits. The unit I gave Tannen is a more sensitive and accurate version. It reads electrical fields in volts per meter and magnetic fields in milligauss. Both are useful in determining spikes in energy or energy lacking an obvious source."

"Cool," Dunlap said, taking it in. "So, what would you normally see with that?"

"Well, in most cases, we would see a bounce near an electrical panel or poorly shielded wiring. In that sense, used to prove "feelings" of discomfort or paranoia have a real-world scientific rationale," the Wally answered.

"So, you use it to disprove claims of those feelings if you see high EMF due to leaky electrical appliances," Dunlap speculated.

"In this house, with the electricity turned off, it should be relatively flat-lined. There are natural causes of EMF, but generally, they don't register very high," Chase added.

"So then if we see high EMF..." Dunlap concluded.

Nodding, Wally completed the agent's thought, "Could be paranormal."

Jeffers rolled his eyes in response to the dialogue. "Can we get going now?"

Stomping up the steps, the senior agent led the way. Barely a hand on the knob, the door popped open. Swinging wide in a terrible whine, Jeffers pushed it all the way open. As soon as it opened, a blast of wind slammed the door back shut on the crew. This time, putting his shoulder into it, Jeffers pushed his way into the foyer.

A rush of curiosity took hold of the remaining five investigators, pushing forward, they all crowded in behind Jeffers. For a few moments of silence, they all listened. Instinctively, Jeffers allowed his hand to brush against his left side, nudging his holster. Chase took the lead, pointing Wally and Don to scan opposing walls they walked. Readying his flashlight, Chase found it was mostly unnecessary. While the narrow hall was gloomy, there was enough late afternoon sun streaking through the dust-caked windows.

With little by way of furnishings, their pace was brisk, moving down the hall and spilling into the kitchen. A single porcelain sink flanked by plain cabinets and an old gas stove that had been disconnected and pulled from the wall made up the simple space. Jeffers moved to the window in front of the sink. Smearing a layer of dust around the glass, he peered out. A wide arch of corn stalks circled the old farmhouse. "They sure take their fear seriously," he muttered.

Professor Chase looked at his compatriots. "Anything?" he asked while snapping a photo of his team in action.

Don shook his head, "Pretty flat. Even the electrical wires are dead. I was sure the power had been cut."

Nodding, Wally agreed, "Same here with the KII. Good baseline."

The tech moved over to the opposite wall. Finding the pantry ajar, Wally pulled it all the way open. Craning his neck, he fumbled for his flashlight and thrust the KII in front of him. Before he could click the flashlight on, the LEDs on the KII strobed, illuminating the storeroom in a colorful arch. Wally's heart raced, instinctively, he hopped backward in momentary panic. Forcing himself, he strode forward, the whole time, the KII reaching its limit.

"Chase, quick, get a picture. KII's spiking off the charts!" Wally called, unable to hide the excitement in his voice.

"Whatcha got there, geek?" Jeffers asked, he too shone his light around the room.

"KII hit. In a house without electricity, it *has* to be an anomalous phenomenon!" Wally declared.

"Or," Chase's calm voice said from behind them, "An FBI agent with his cellphone on."

Wally's face turned red as Agent Jeffers pulled his smartphone from his pocket, looking at it questioningly. Frustrated, Wally waved the KII at the phone. The lights again went ballistic. Moving the EMF detector away from the agent and back to the pantry, the lights went dead.

"Should have asked you guys to turn off your phones or place them by the entrance. Helps rule out accidental hits like that one," Chase conceded, "As Wally opened the door, Agent Jeffers followed and was looking over his shoulder, right then, KII hit."

Dunlap pulled his phone out and powered it down. Agent Sohn looked at her phone and back at Chase quizzically. Reluctantly, she retired her phone to the front door.

As the afternoon sun dipped toward the horizon, the angles for light became less prevalent. Chase glanced at his watch, "It is going to get dark pretty quick. We might as well break and grab the gear while we have light."

"You guys need help?" Agent Dunlap asked.

"We'll take all we can get," Chase agreed.

The platoon moved back out of the house and down the rickety steps. Opening the back of the van, Wally began unloading case after case of equipment. One by one, Chase and Tannen carried them into the house. Dunlap and Agent Sohn snatched up gear and followed. Agent Jeffers just gawked, open-mouthed, "How much crap do you nerds have? Is this really all necessary?"

"No," Wally shrugged, "We could all hold hands in front of an Ouija board and call out names three times in a row."

Special Agent Jeffers wrinkled his nose.

"He's kidding. We don't do Ouijas or séances. If we want to get to a scientific conclusion or at least rule out natural explanations, this is the equipment to do it with. We'll get this done quicker if you help," Chase said, grabbing a second load of gear.

Begrudgingly, Jeffers grabbed a Pelican case. "What is all this anyway?" he complained.

"Infrared cameras, motion detectors, trap cameras, laser grids, portable weather station, FLIR camera- the usual," Chase shrugged.

"You have a FLIR?" Jeffers asked, astonished.

"It's my favorite. Aside from voice recorders, probably the most useful in picking up evidence," the professor nodded.

"This is going to be weird," the agent muttered.

"You can use the FLIR if you want," Chase offered. For the first time, he picked up a hint of interest from Jeffers.

With the pile of gear lining the hallway, the paranormal investigators began setting up a command post. The FBI agents watched as the trio scurried around, placing cameras and stringing cords. Wally disappeared, backing out of the house with a reel of extension cord. Soon, he came bounding back in.

"I think we're good. Why don't you guys see what we've got," the tech said. Following behind him, the troop huddled around the back of the van. A folding table held a bank of monitors and laptops. Each screen showed a different shot of the house. Some showed the exterior, though most were of the interior of the house.

"Looks good, Wally. Why don't you walk us through what you have?" Chase admired. "The main screen shows the four DVR cameras split out. This shot is the kitchen. This is the stairs. We have the upstairs hallway, and this shot down the steps into the storm cellar. This monitor shows the quadrant of the motion detectors. If any of its beams are broken, its section will light up and blink. This one splits the front and rear of the outside of the house. We don't have specific claims since…well…since the witness are all dead," Wally said, pointing to the screens.

"Home, sweet home," Don Tannen smiled.

"Don usually stays in the van and monitors things. As the medic, he can keep an eye on us and come in if we need help," Chase explained.

"We have our FRS radios so that we can stay in contact," Don added, patting his against his side.

"You guys are welcome to stay in here with Tannen or join Wally and me in the house," Chase offered.

"I'm in. Can I use the EMF thing?" Agent Dunlap asked.

"I'm going to do a perimeter sweep and gut the house, just to make sure there aren't *real* things here that might cause you harm," Jeffers said, "Then, I'll join the medic and take a snooze until you are all done communing with the dead."

"Agent Sohn?" Chase raised his eyebrows.

"I think I'll run the sweep with Jeffers and then run security. You say I can monitor most of the house from your command post?"

"Yep."

"Alright, the sun's about to set. We might as well go dark," Chase said. Checking his flashlight, grabbing a voice recorder, and an infrared camera, he followed Wally back into the house.

Jeffers led Agent Sohn into the house as well, making a beeline for the basement. "Probably some vagrant who's whacking people who are homing in on his free rent," the senior agent suggested.

Each step down the stairs emitted a harsh squeal as the old wood strained to support the agents. "So much for the element of surprise," Danica remarked.

Both agents swung their lights in opposing arcs, ensuring each shadow was uncovered. Their eyes scanned for signs of movement. The basement held a sundry of discarded farm equipment. Most rusted and broken. The odd shapes cast eerie shadows on the wall. Agent Sohn did her best to ignore them, her training encouraging her to only focus on actual movement. Together, they searched every inch of the basement, coming up empty.

"No doubt someone comes in here, they're going to feel creeped out," Sohn shared.

"I suppose," Jeffers shrugged.

"Come on, none of this bothers you?"

The senior agent looked at her for a moment before answering, "The truth is, I've seen some of the worst in real live human beings. Case two years ago, a terror squad seeking out buildings with daycares attached because they thought they'd be higher yield soft targets. One of my first assignments– an interstate serial murderer preying on college freshman. The case right before you came on, I busted a diplomat who was selling secrets to the Middle East. No, some creep in an old farmhouse does not bother me."

"You resent being here, with Dr. Chase and his men," Agent Sohn stated, "I see your perspective. There is another way to look at it. I researched his work before coming out here. He seems like a respectable man. His science is good, if the area he studies is a bit fringe."

"With all respect, I can see sending Dunlap or another junior agent out here, but…there are more important things the bureau needs to focus on with its resources," Jeffers sighed. Abandoning the basement, they retreated to the main floor. There they found Chase and Wally asking questions to a voice recorder. The professor paused the device as the agents walked up.

"Find anything?" Chase asked.

"Just a slew of tetanus cases waiting to happen," Jeffers retorted.

"We'll check upstairs and then leave the house to you and your team," Sohn added.

"Sounds good. I appreciate you being here," Chase said as he headed upstairs with another piece of equipment.

Nodding, the agents made their way up the steps. On each floor, the agents took the role of security seriously, shining their lights in every room and looking behind each door. Reaching the third floor, they met up with Agent Dunlap and Wally. "Clean so far," Jeffers noted.

"Here too," Dunlap exclaimed, holding an EMF detector in the air.

Jeffers shook his head in disgust as the rookie agent worked with the paranormal investigators. "Dunlap, how about you make yourself genuinely useful and climb up into the attic. That is the last place we need to check before we can lock the place down and consider it safe for Dr. Chase and his crew to…to do whatever it is they do," Jeffers commanded.

Nodding, the junior agent found the small overhead panel that led to the attic. Jumping up, he grabbed the sill of the opening and pulled himself up into the attic. A bat swept by causing Dunlap to duck before it fluttered through a large crack along one of the eaves. "We are not alone here!"

"What is it, see something?" Wally called back eagerly.

Instinctively, Agent Jeffers rested his hand on his holster.

"Bats. Pretty good evidence there is a family of them in here."

"Colony," Chase nodded absently, as he joined the party on the upper floor.

"Otherwise, it's clear!" Dunlap's feet appeared in the opening.

"Hey, Dunlap, how about you place one of these cameras up there while you're up there?" Wally held a trap camera up to the hole. The agent's hand reached down and grabbed it. "Just push the orange button and place it somewhere you can see most of the attic with." The tech seemed please he wouldn't have to find a way up into the space himself.

"Come on, let's get out of here," Jeffers grumbled.

"You'll secure the perimeter?" Chase asked.

"The only way in will be the front, where we will have eyes," the lead agent replied.

"Excellent, let's get to work," Chase nodded.

FOUR

The Helberg house was locked down. Apart from the entrance, and cameras or motion alarms monitoring the rear and the sides, nothing would get in or out without the investigation team knowing. Don Tannen sat in the back of the van. Several monitors revealed the variety of camera views covering each floor of the house. Agent Sohn joined him, studying each shot as it was fed back to the LCDs. In the SUV next to them, Agent Jeffers pulled out his laptop and worked through his backlog of reports.

In the foyer, Dr. Chase laid out the team's gear. One by one, he and Wally explained to Agent Dunlap how each instrument was used. A handful of voice recorders, hand-held cameras capable of taking pictures at night. Equipment for recording temperature and wind. When Chase got to the FLIR, Dunlap's eyes lit up.

"That's one of our favorite units. Taking pictures by using heat signatures, an entity invisible to the human eyes, but made up of either colder or warmer energy, would be picked up by this. These cameras have captured some of the most compelling evidence," Chase said.

"Sweet! Can I use it?" the agent asked.

"Sure," Chase shrugged.

"It is a very expensive piece of equipment," Wally warned the agent.

"Got it," Dunlap nodded. "Where do we start?"

"Let's do a walkthrough. We can review the prior cases. Then, just like when you're hunting for bad guys, we'll do a sweep."

"Let's go!" Dunlap urged.

Wally picked up a handheld video camera affixed with a bank of infrared lights and followed Dunlap and Chase down the hall.

"The latest case," Chase reported, half to Dunlap and half to the camera, "involved a local man, quite familiar with the house and its history. No one knows why he came in here that afternoon about two weeks ago. When he didn't come home, and his dog was found wandering through town, a search by the local sheriff's office brought them here. They found him dead right about…there!" Chase pointed to the floor in front of the pantry.

Both Wally and Agent Dunlap directed their cameras to the floor and then up at the closed door of the pantry. "I thought this was open earlier," Chase said. Reaching for the handle of the closet, the three men steadied themselves. A rustle from inside made the tension in the air bristle. Turning the knob, the old door bellowed a loud groan as the professor pulled.

Snapping the beam of his flashlight, Chase moved it quickly about the closet. Catching movement, he swung it wildly into the corner, the cameras following his light. Barely in the cast of the beam, two deep red eyes stared back at them. Just as the corner was illuminated, they saw a tail slip through a slit where the wall and floor met. Letting out a breath and almost laughing in partial relief and disappointment, he declared, "A rat!"

"Got him!" Wally tapped the camera.

"The life of a paranormal investigator," Chase confessed to the agent. "Let's finish our walkthrough."

Leading the way up the stairs, ignoring the complaints issued by the old steps, he shared, "A group of teenagers had snuck in about a month ago. One of them left the group to relieve himself. The group heard him scream, and he bolted past them, right down these steps and out the door. They found him on the side of the road about a mile towards town. He died of cardiac arrest." Guiding them to the bathroom, long since non-functioning. The fixtures were still intact, though stained brown from standing water. A tarnished mirror leaned against the wall behind the basin.

"Another incident from within the house occurred when two local farmers were working the field outback. They heard sounds coming from the house. When they came in to investigate, they heard what sounded like footsteps in the hallway. When they came up the steps, one of the men screamed, clutched his chest, and turned to his friend. He went dead weight, nearly knocking the both of them down the stairwell. The friend carried him out to the porch. He rode his tractor to his house and called for help, by the time they arrived, the man was dead. That was the first victim," Chase said.

"I thought there were six deaths?" Dunlap questioned.

"The town has attributed three more to the house. Two people who drove by the house and died in town shortly after. A third who was an unfortunate census aide who had stopped to make sure no one lived here anymore. That person survived all the way back to town, making a few additional stops and died in his hotel room that night. He had been talking to the bartender about the 'creepy house' out on the highway."

"Ever investigate anything like this professor? With people dying?" the agent asked.

Locking on Dunlap's eyes, Chase replied, "No."

"This area has two counts of reports, might as well do an EVP," Wally declared, sitting in the hallway cross-legged. Switching on a voice recorder, the ghost hunter placed it on the floor. "Anybody got a dime?"

Dunlap fished in his pockets, "Here, why?"

Holding up a plastic device, "This KII unit has a push button you have to hold, but we find it works well to have it on consistently. If I jam a coin in it, I can force the button depressed and voila, hands-free."

"Ok, what do you hope to get with it sitting here?" the agent asked.

"It is a simple EMF scanner. Like the device you were scanning with earlier. This one is not as accurate, but with its yellow, red, green light display, it makes it easy to see," the tech explained.

"It even allows us to have yes/no binary response conversations," Chase added.

"Wow, conversations? Cool," the agent said excitedly and then frowned, "How does that work?"

"We ask questions and ask for a specific response to the meter- make it flash twice, that sort of thing. Then we ask follow up questions to rule out some fluke EMF fluctuation," Wally shared.

"Let's get going," Chase said, as Dunlap studied the KII. Speaking into the tiny voice recorder, the professor kicked off the session, "This is Ryder, Wally, and Agent Dunlap starting EVP in the upstairs hallway of the Helberg house. Is there anyone with us?"

After a pause, he continued, "Are there more than one of you?"

"Do you know that you're scaring people, even possibly hurting them?"

"Are you Mr. Helberg? Or a member of the Helberg family?"

Wally interjected, "You can talk to us. See the device with the little red light? That can record your voice, even if we can't hear it, it will capture it. The thing next to it lights up if you go up to it. It is another way you can communicate with us."

"You *do* have a story to tell, don't you?" Chase asked.

Intently, the three listened in silence. Only the soft breeze and the occasional crack of the old house settling broke the stillness.

After minutes of hush and pointing the FLIR camera in is hand around the hallway, Dunlap asked, "Now what?"

"This is how it goes. Think of it like being on a stakeout," Chase said. "We'll move to a different spot in a few minutes."

"Alright," Dunlap said. Standing up, he crept down the hall, disappearing into the various rooms, peering through the darkness with the colorful display of the FLIR. As he entered investigated the rooms, he felt like the air around him had grown even more stale. Pulling at his collar, he cleared his throat.

Poking his head into the bathroom where the teenager had allegedly fled from, he sat on the edge of the claw foot bathtub. Swiping his wrist across his forehead, he wondered how it had gotten so hot, with the sun long since set.

Undoing a button on his shirt, he concentrated on the screen. For a second, he thought the colors on the screen had changed. Only briefly, the screen looked like the wispy mirage that heat makes off of pavement on a summer day. He looked again; it was normal.

About to return to the paranormal crew, his eye caught something in the corner of the room. Just behind the basin, something flashed past the mirror. Standing up, he approached slowly, his heart began to pound at his chest, his skin felt like it was boiling, yet a shiver overcame him as he shuddered. Glancing at the mirror, he spun the FLIR in the opposite direction, where whatever the reflection would have actually been. Unable to resist, he readied his firearm with his free hand.

He wanted to call out to Dr. Chase and Wally, but all that escaped was a raspy whisper. Moving towards the hallway, he froze. Blocking the doorway was a large shadow looming directly in front of him. He glanced at the FLIR that flickered and suddenly shut off. Dunlap's chest tightened, he felt his legs wobble. The agent had to strain his vision as he concentrated on the shape in his path, trying to identify it. Lowering a shoulder, Dunlap lunged forward, driving through the mass that blocked his way. Slipping clean through the doorway and across the hall, the agent slammed into the wall. His head spun, his pulse raged through his veins, and his world slipped away into blackness.

Ryder Chase sat still, listening for a response. He strained his eyes, trying to make out shapes in the hallway, but save for the light on the voice recorder. He was greeted only by darkness. "Give us a sign, and we'll leave you alone for the night."

As his words entered the still of the night, an eruption of bangs and slams rang from the hallway. Both Chase and Wally spun, snapping their flashlights on in the direction of the hall. Neither expected to see a solid mass, melting to the floor.

Chase scrambled to his feet and raced down the hall. Sliding on his knees, he stopped at the fallen heap of Agent Dunlap. Gently rolling the agent on his back, the professor found the man unresponsive. With his pointer and index fingers, he found the agent's carotid artery and searched for vitals. Chase found the man's skin hot to the touch, his pulse non-existent.

"Call Tannen, get him up here right now!" Chase spat at his lead investigator.

Wally pressed the button on his walkie, "Don, we need you right away. Something has happened to Agent Dunlap. He is out cold on the floor. I don't know, Ryder is with him."

Within moments, the front door crashed open, and the sound of several sets of footprints echoed through the old farmhouse. Agent Jeffers appeared first in the hallway, followed by Agent Sohn and Don Tannen laboring behind, lugging his EMS pack.

"What happened?" Jeffers demanded.

Ryder Chase shook his head, "I don't know. Agent Dunlap was exploring the rooms up here, suddenly Wally and I heard a crash and found him slumped on the floor."

"Got a pulse?" Tannen asked as he knelt beside the agent.

"No, I couldn't find one. And his skin…unusually warm," Chase answered.

Tannen checked for a pulse himself, "He *is* really warm." Checking Dunlap's breathing, the EMT shook his head. Diving into his pack, he produced an automated external defibrillator and began gathering readings. "He's in arrest." Tannen set to deliver a shock. The first wave spiked. Nothing for a moment. Tannen readied a second shock when the device picked up a pulse. Slow at first, but then it steadily began to rise.

Tannen watched intently as the agent's lungs began to pump, gasps of air gurgled out of his throat, and he began to climb back to life. Checking his watch, the medic calculated how much time likely elapsed. Outside, an ambulance wailed as it pulled alongside the old house.

Jeffers and Sohn looked on as Tanned worked. Seeing their worry, the EMT spoke, "He's going to be okay. I don't know why his heart would have stopped, but he'll be okay."

Dunlap's eyes opened suddenly, wide and with a start that made the AED scream before he recognized the people around him. Sputtering, he tried to speak, but Tannen urged him to be calm. The ambulance personnel had been led up the stairs by Wally and made their way with the transport gurney.

"Cardiac arrest. The victim had no pulse and had stopped breathing. With the AED, I administered one series of shock, and he came back. Victim has elevated skin temperature and is stressed," Tannen told the ambulance crew as they loaded the agent.

The responder nodded, "We got him. Hospital in Fargo has a good cardio unit."

Jeffers and Sohn followed the ambulance crew down the stairs and out to the waiting van.

In the hallway, Ryder Chase looked at his two associates as Tannen packed his gear. "What the hell is going on here?"

FIVE

With Agent Dunlap en route to the hospital, the investigators returned to the upstairs hallway. Wally had gathered the gear that had scattered on the floor when the agent collapsed. Inspecting each piece as the remaining team decided on a course of action. "We are all worried about Agent Dunlap. Let's try and see if we can figure out what happened to him, and then let's wrap up for the night. I am sure our concern for him is paramount."

"Well, he had just come out of this room here," Wally said, shining his light into the bathroom.

Agent Jeffers stood in the doorway. Carefully, he played his light around every inch of the small room. Judiciously covering all of the fixtures. "Any signs of injury?"

"No, not that I could tell," Chase shook his head.

"Me either. Just seemed like a classic myochardial infarction, just with a young, fit agent," Tannen agreed.

"One who had not long ago completed the Bureau's medical ringer," Jeffers sighed.

"Did you guys hear anything? Did he say anything?" Danica Sohn asked.

"Not really. We were doing an EVP right over there," Chase pointed, "Pretty quiet until we heard Dunlap in the hall, and he and the gear drop to the floor."

"What gear did he have?" Agent Sohn asked.

"Voice recorder and the FLIR," Wally replied.

"That FLIR record stuff?"

"Yeah, if you pull the trigger. Kind of like a point and shoot camera, the way it was rigged, it was set to capture a still," Wally answered and then looked annoyed at himself, "We should check it." Pulling up the screen on the handheld thermal camera, the tech began flashing through the last captured images. Most were random shots of the bathroom, the cooler porcelain clearly defined in the colorful pictures.

"Wait, go back!" Agent Sohn snapped.

Wally reversed the screen a slide.

"What is that?" Sohn, held a finger to the edge of the screen.

The entire group crowded around the three-inch screen.

"Is that…a person?" Sohn felt the hair on the back of her neck stand up. Agent Jeffers cocked his head, trying to rationalize what he was seeing. A muted orange shape lined the right edge of the image. It appeared like half a person peering out at the camera.

Chase swept his flashlight in the direction he figured the shot had been taken. His beam covered the door jam and the corner of the room near the washbasin. Working the light around the area, suddenly he saw a flash. Moving the light back, the room lit slightly. Training his flashlight squarely on the space, he muttered, "Mirror. It's hard to tell, but it is possible what we see in the still is a reflection."

Wally moved the switch to capture and held the FLIR in the direction of the image. Slowly circling the room, he vaguely caught a similar shape, though the color didn't quite match. "I don't know, can't be sure."

"Ugh, you losers nearly had me thinking for a minute," Jeffers snapped.

"*Something* affected your agent. There is no one else in here. The building was secure…" Chase began.

Tannen snapped his fingers excitedly, "The surveillance video. We have a camera in the hallway. Maybe it will show us what happened!"

The group rushed down the steps and towards the paranormal team's van. Focusing on the monitors, Tannen searched the files until he found the time segment when Agent Dunlap stumbled into the hall. As they watched the replay, they saw an empty corridor. Suddenly Dunlap burst into frame. Panic was etched in the agent's face as he careened out of the bathroom and into the hall. He dropped the FLIR as he clutched his chest, slamming full force into the wall on the far side of the hallway. In a mortal collapse, he crashed to the floor.

"Play it back," Jeffers demanded.

Tannen clicked back to the start and looped the video. Again, they watched Dunlap emerge and fall to the floor.

"See that? He looks back, like as if someone is there!" Jeffers shouted.

"But we were all on the scene. We checked out the room. No one came in or out," Sohn declared.

"Even if there was a person up there, who would frighten your agent so much?" Wally asked.

Jeffers shrugged, "He's only worked a handful of cases since the academy. Add in all your mumbo jumbo, who knows?"

"I'm not sure. Wouldn't we have seen someone?" Chase argued.

"Let's recheck that room. Any possible exits, the window, a vent…anything." The agent took the lead and marched back into the Helberg House. Everyone but Tannen followed who quickly locked himself in the van to continue monitoring the equipment, unnerved to be out in the night alone.

Back in the bathroom, Jeffers made a beeline for the window.

"We have an exterior camera on all sides of the house," Wally said behind the agent who ignored him.

Jeffers panned his flashlight along the sill and tried the window. The window refused to budge. Years of neglect, humidity, and dust locked the frame in place. Freeing the latch on the lock, the agent tried the window again.

"Uhm, so someone crawled in the window, frightened your agent, left by the window, and somehow locked it behind them?" Wally scoffed.

Jeffers pounded his fist along the frame, flakes of aged paint crumbling to the floor. Suddenly he thrust the window open. Turning to the team, which was now staring at his antics, "Well, now we know the window opens."

Chase shone his light around the room again. "There's no vent, only the one window and the one door." Walking to the window, he stood beside Agent Jeffers and then stuck his head out of the window. "And jumped twenty feet to the ground. The rear of the house is a flat façade. Anyone see someone sneak up to the house with a ladder tonight?" Chase moved his light back in forth along the ground outside of the house. A scraping sound caught his ear, just as Jeffers grabbed him and yanked him into the room. As Chase cleared the window, the frame slammed shut.

"Thing was like a guillotine!" Wally exclaimed.

"Holy...thanks Agent Jeffers," Chase choked.

"I know that sound. The same thing used to happen at my grandmas. Over the years, the windows just don't fit like they used to. I had my hands whacked a few too many times," the agent replied.

"I don't know what Agent Dunlap saw or thought he saw. I can't explain it," Chase shrugged.

"I can," Jeffers snapped, "Seeded by notions from the town, an old house in the middle of nowhere and so-called expertise on spooky things heightens your stressors. Throw in a willing believer, and you have a simple case of mind over matter."

"I can't deny much of what you said. We see that all the time in people. It doesn't match up with the number of occurrences and terrible results of the victims, though," Chase conceded.

"Well, I can say that there is nothing here now," Jeffers rubbed his neck, the long day and stress of his subordinate in the cardio unit weighing on him.

"We can wrap up for the tonight. Why don't you guys check on Agent Dunlap?" Chase offered.

"Reconvene in the morning? I saw a little diner across from Town Hall," Agent Sohn suggested.

The paranormal crew nodded and began the process of breaking down their gear. While they wrapped their cords, grabbed their recording devices and cameras, they kept a keen ear for anything out of place. In short work, they had their gear stowed in the rear of the van with no new disturbances to report.

SIX

Wally Smyth stumbled into his hotel room, exhausted from the travel and excitement at the Helberg House. Rubbing his eyes, he sat on the edge of his bed, flipping through the channels on the hotel TV. Landing on SYFY Channel, he let the program run in the background as he performed his nightly duties. He began by setting out his laptop and plugging in several USB-based connections to download much of their evidence directly to the hard drive.

Brushing his teeth, he spat the water back in the sink. Wrinkling his nose, he flicked his tongue through his teeth, trying to dispatch the taste of the town's water. He was always sensitive to local water when he traveled.

Grabbing his now warm tea from the bedside stand, he took several big gulps and settled in for the night. As his head hit the pillow, he was out cold- the post-apocalyptic movie still running in the background.

Wally didn't know how long he had been asleep. He woke, feeling his body was on fire. Kicking off the sheets, he shot up out of bed. The television playing an infomercial suddenly switched to static. The clamorous noise rang in Wally's ears, causing him to scramble for the remote.

Diving on the bed, he grabbed desperately towards the bed stand. As he moved his finger to the off button, he froze. The static had become an irregular pattern. The tech's hair on the back of his neck stood high as he recognized voices in the static. He couldn't make out what they were saying at first. Then the voices become more clear- not perfect, but like an AM station as you're passing through a tunnel.

He stared at the grey fuzz as he listened. "Get out!" the television hissed. "It's…. coming. Go…." Bolting to the window, Wally threw the curtains aside, what he saw nearly knocked him to the floor. The streets were filled with people. Horrified people who appeared to be running for their lives. As a woman passed by his window, she turned to him, her hair flowing as she ran. He locked his eyes with hers. They were vacant, dark blue abysses. Tears ran from where her eyes should have been. Then she was gone, focused on her flight. She disappeared into the night.

Wally's heart raced. He fought to turn the lock on the door and flung it open. Darting out of his room, he pounded on the door next to him. Flailing at the door, he nearly hit Ryder Chase as he opened it and greeted his friend.

"Wally, what is it? What's going on?" Chase asked sleepily.

"The people, did you see the people?" Wally asked.

"What people?"

"In the street, they were running, all of them running," Wally stammered, "Their eyes, they weren't right. And the T. V.…. the voices."

"You heard voices through the television?" Chase repeated.

"Everything alright in here?" Don Tannen's voice asked from the adjacent doorway.

"Wally came in, he's pretty stressed," Chase replied. "Did you see any people in the street?"

"No," Tannen shook his head as he darted to Wally's side. Maneuvering the agitated man to the edge of the bed, he stated, "You're burning up!"

Placing his fingers against his wrist, "And your pulse is way up. I better get my bag. Sit here. I'll be right back." The EMT moved quickly out of the room.

Watching his friend beginning to calm down, Chase asked, "You alright, man?"

"I…I think so," Wally nodded. His eyes looked vague. His skin turned nearly grey.

In moments, Tannen dashed back into the room. Once more, his AED rendered into service. "Wally's vitals are a bit out of whack, but I think he'll be okay," the EMT announced, reading the results of the screen, "We should probably move you to the local hospital for observation."

"No, I'll be okay."

"Well, I have a spare queen in my room. At least try and get some sleep in there, that way if anything changes, I'll be right there," Tannen suggested.

"I'm a big boy, I…"

"That or the hospital," Tannen pressed.

"Fine. Daylight isn't going to give us any more time 'cause we're arguing," Wally relented.

"Give me a call if anything happens," Chase said as the other two men left his room.

Turning the deadbolt, the weary professor shuffled back to his bed and snatched off the light. Unable to resist, he slid the curtains of his hotel room aside, just to see if he would find any of Wally's people running down the street. Satisfied the town of Hope was as quiet as the late hour dictated, he retired to his bed.

Sleep did not come easy to the professor. His mind worked overtime to reason an explanation for the events that night. First, Agent Dunlap, then Wally. Both lucky to have Tannen close by, or who knows how they would have fared. What in the world did those two men really see? And Wally here at the hotel, not at Helberg House. Chase finally gave in to exhaustion, arresting his mind from further contemplation, hoping the answers could be found in the evidence review the next day. Through the slit in the hotel room curtains, he could see tomorrow was not at all far away.

SEVEN

Wally Smyth woke disoriented. Opening his eyes, seeing the unmade bed across the room took a moment to register in his head. Then he remembered the crazy procession through town he had witnessed and Tannen's ultimate insistence that he be monitored the rest of the night. Sitting up, he felt a slight tug at his chest and realized his EMT buddy had left the monitoring probes on him overnight.

Ripping the mild adhesive off, he yawned. Other than feeling like he had a slight hangover, he otherwise felt fine. Standing up, he made his way to the door of the hotel room. Outside, the sun was already up and quickly warming Hope's streets. Making his way to his own room, he found the door unlocked from his hasty exit and went in.

For some reason, he was tentative at entering. He cast the television a suspicious glare. Smacking his parched mouth, he searched for a cup. Grabbing his tea from the day before, he let the liquid coat his mouth. The flavor had decidedly changed for the worst, and he dumped the rest in the sink.

Snapping on the shower, he splashed water over his face and let the steam complete his reanimation to the living.

Ryder Chase pulled his headphones off as Don Tannen was tapping wildly on his shoulder. "Listen to this. It is about the time Agent Dunlap collapsed in the hall."

Ryder swapped headphones with the EMT and nodded. The audio was the static voice recorder they had placed in the second-floor hallway. He could faintly hear himself and Tannen holding their EVP further down the hall. Suddenly a gasp very close to the recorder could be heard. A voice that was indistinguishable for ownership rasped, "Who's there? Help…help me!" The voice was followed by the sound of Dunlap's equipment clattering. Soon, loud footsteps, plastic, and metal slamming to the floor with a crescendo of the sickening thud of the agent's body crashing in the hall resounded through the earpieces.

Replaying the segment several times, Chase shook his head, "I definitely hear it. Can't be sure who it is on the recording. Could be Agent Dunlap, might not be. Go ahead and mark it." Ryder slapped his headphones back over his ears and stared at the screen in front of him. He was reviewing the footage from the FLIR thermal camera, making sure they didn't miss anything from the quick review they ran during the night. Frame by frame, he zoomed in questionable sections of each shot, none showing anything conclusive.

Feeling as though he were being watched, Ryder Chase turned to see Don staring at him. Once more, Chase removed his headphones.

"Here is the footage from the surveillance camera on the second floor. I have rewound it to the period just before we found Agent Dunlap."

At first, the hall beyond the two running their EVP session was dark and empty. Suddenly darts of light slashed their way out of the bathroom, erratically playing into the camera shot of the hallway. Chase wrinkled his nose, "It's weird, almost like there is a struggle going on."

"Yeah, that's kind of what I saw too. Very strange. And then…here comes Agent Dunlap. He looks desperate."

"And horrified," added Chase.

"Then he's down."

"Rewind?" Chase requested.

Tannen clicked the mouse and moved the video bar a few seconds.

"It almost looks like a shadow here." Chase pointed at the screen with a pen. "But like the audio, hard to pin it on anything other than maybe Dunlap himself."

"Hopefully, he has made a full recovery and can shed some light," Tannen nodded.

"Hopefully," Chase agreed. "I'll go down to the hospital and give our well-wishes, why don't you check on Wally."

"No need," a voice came from the doorway. "Wally is here, and he feels fit for duty."

Chase raised an eyebrow, "Not so sure. Forget about your near-death experience last night, but you, Wally, seem to be speaking in third person."

"Just for effect, boss," the tech grinned. "I'll take over your seat. Anything interesting?"

"Interesting, but not definitive. Nothing I could argue without the shadow of a doubt. So, in the light of the day, what do you think about last night?"

Wally shook his head, his face in a scowl, "I really don't know what to think. A dream? Some feverish delirium? I gotta be honest, I was hoping our resident med-tech might have some insight."

"Well, you *were* feverish. That certainly could be it. Two separate auditory and visual hallucinations…man, that's pretty wild," Tannen said.

"It sure seemed real. I was genuinely sphincter-clenching scared," Wally admitted.

"In all the situations we have been in, I have never known you to fear anything," Chase added.

"Me either," Tannen echoed.

"I guess we will see what tonight holds," Wally shrugged.

Chase and Tannen nodded. The professor filled Wally in on the segments that still needed review and relinquished his seat. Wally slapped on a pair of headphones and clicked play on the computer screen. Chase studied his friend for a moment, ensuring he truly was well enough to be up.

Tannen seemed to be reading Chase's mind. Giving him a reassuring nod, the professor could leave knowing Wally was in good hands.

The Fargo Medical Center seemed different to Chase. Even at the university hospital where he worked, there was constantly an air of frenzy. Here, the scene was unique. It seemed calm to him, at least in comparison. Overhearing staff conversations, he didn't get the impression they were any less competent, just merely calm.

In control. Perhaps what is the differentiator of families living in the country's core versus the coastlines.

Agent Sohn greeted him outside one of the many diverging hallways. She looked tired, slight darkening under her usually bright green eyes. Her hair tousled, and her pantsuit wrinkled, she somehow still managed an imposingly attractive presence. Despite Wally's rants about her, it was the first time that Ryder Chase noticed her as anything other than an FBI agent. Perhaps because of the innocence of the circumstances, she struck him a bit differently. Her human side, her genuine femininity, was allowed past her professional persona. Here in the hallway, she was soft and kind, yet maintained her serious and undeniably commanding air.

"Dr. Chase?" Sohn called, she crooked her head and raised her eyebrow.

Chase shook himself, his cheeks reddening at how lost in his thoughts he was. Suddenly, he wondered if he had been gawking at her. "Sorry," he shuffled his foot, "It was a long night for all of us."

The agent cast him a curious look.

"Not as crucial as finding out about Agent Dunlap," Chase waved her expression off, "Though perhaps related. How *is* Agent Dunlap?"

"He had some rough spots between the farmhouse and the hospital. They removed him from Cardiac-ICU early this morning, and he is in recovery. Exhausted, but otherwise fine. Doc said Tannen probably saved his life," Sohn shared. "The cardiologist is baffled. Agent Dunlap is in great shape, no family history. There was no medical rationale that makes sense."

"Hmm. Any other avenues he recommended to explore?"

"Pharmacological...and."

"And?"

"Psychiatric," Sohn said.

"Psych?"

"We'll cross that one after the tox scan," the agent shrugged. "Sudden cardiac events can occur due to neurological abnormalities. Preliminary results don't show anything, though."

"I'm glad he's going to be okay. Is there anything we can do for him?" Chase asked.

"I think he'd like for you to figure out what the heck is going on out at that house," Agent Sohn looked deliberate in her response.

Chase nodded, "We'll do everything we can."

Wally and Tannen remained parked in front of the monitors; headphones clamped to their ears. Chase tapped Wally, "You okay?"

"I'm fine," Wally nodded and slapped the earpiece back over his ear.

Tannen nodded to confirm, "He seems back to normal, well, as normal as Wally gets, at least."

"Anything new in the results?" Chase nodded at the pile of notes in front of the EMT.

"Some odds and ends. Sounds, tapping, shuffling on the recorders, a handful of photos with shadows, light streaks and orbs," Tannen shrugged.

Chase frowned, "You know how I feel about orbs."

Orbs or balls of light captured in photos have been a staple of paranormal investigations. Highly debated in the culture as proponents declare them to be light energy denoting a spirit while others, Chase included, remand them to being mere specs of dust or flying insects that stream close to the lens.

"I know," Tannen nodded, "I'm just noting the ones that correlate with events or noises."

"If you feel you must," Chase commented as he retreated to his room to jump on a department conference call.

Every moment of the night before had been combed through – every piece of audio, every video segment. Hours ticked by, the team jotting down notations for items they wanted to review in greater detail.

The teleconference had ended minutes before Chase realized it was over. Leaning back against the desk chair, he had been engrossed in thinking through the case. He hadn't heard a moment of the conference call other than to announce himself present. Clicking the phone off, he hurried to find his partners.

Every moment of the night before had been combed through and each instrument's data analyzed. Hours ticked by, the team jotting down notations for items they wanted to review in greater detail.

"Did we get anything else?" he asked as he burst into Tannen's room.

The medic looked up at Chase. "Well, you know about the FLIR with Agent Dunlap. We blew it up on the big monitor. It seems weird, but hard to say." The EMT pushed play on the recording and showed it. Without asking for it, he backed it up and let it play at a frame a second.

Chase shook his head, "Yeah, really hard to tell. Agent Dunlap certainly seemed odd with his reactions holding it, but I can't make anything out from the video."

"We couldn't either," Wally admitted. "There is a fringe by the door frame, but that could have been a quick variation from movement. Don, play the footage from cam three next."

Tannen cued up the security camera file. "There! Did you see that?"

"Let me see that again," Chase requested.

Tannen looped it and hit play. Shooting down the main hallway, the shot captured a part of a window. At one point, it seemed as if the little bit of light let through it was briefly covered.

After watching it again, Chase muttered, scratching his chin, "I don't have an answer for that one. I assume everyone was accounted for?"

"Yeah," Wally nodded.

"We have a few more things," Tannen offered, "Here is a shot from the trap cam we had in the basement. No one was down there, and I can't find anything in the image that would have set it off."

Chase studied the photo of the empty room.

"*Something* had to set it off. If it were a person, they'd be in the shot," Wally shrugged.

Nodding, Chase agreed, "Good anomaly."

Wally floated another photo on the screen. Strange globes hung in the air around the room.

"Orbs again?" Chase asked incredulously, reiterating, "Don't show me orbs."

"But, several paranormal spe-," the tech began to argue.

"No orbs. The way cameras work, dust is too easily reflected. Most reported haunted places have gobs of dust to contribute to the effect. No orbs," Chase demanded.

Wally slumped, "Fine. Don, let him hear the audio."

Through the speakers, the sound hissed as the EMT cranked the volume. After a pause in the echo of footsteps on the floor that Tannen admitted was one of the investigators, they heard a breathy sigh.

"Hard to say," Chase said. "Any more?"

"One last one," Tannen cued up the recorder.

Through the speakers, they heard a child-like voice whisper, "Hello…"

It was enough to send a brief chill up the professor's neck. "That one is interesting. Can you separate that clip and put it in an MP3 file?"

Wally nodded.

"Nice work, guys. Can't say anything we caught is conclusive, but it adds to the stories. Let's pack up, and we'll get ready to head back out there," Chase said.

EIGHT

"Dunlap will be okay, the hospital is going to hold him for one more day under observation, but all tests are coming back clear," Agent Sohn informed the paranormal team. Gathered around their vehicles in the parking lot, the investigators convened.

"That's puzzling," Wally frowned, "But in a good way. You know, yay Agent Dunlap!" The engineer studied the group warily for response.

Special Agent-in-charge Jeffers shot the paranormal researcher a disapproving look.

Sohn broke in, "It *is* an unusual case. The doctors at the hospital are baffled."

"Yeah, but cornfield doctors, does that really qualify as much?" Jeffers quipped.

"I'm glad to hear he's going to be okay," Chase replied.

"Sounds like Mr. Tactful had his own experience," Jeffers nodded towards Wally.

The engineer shrugged, "Probably just a dream, especially after what happened with Dunlap."

"Well, if we can spare any theatrics, let's get back to your investigation. I move that we divide and conquer. You guys need to do whatever it is you do out at that old farmhouse. We need to do real investigative work," Agent Jeffers conferred.

"Sounds good, we are used to working creepy places," Tannen said, his voice not airing a great deal of confidence.

"Unfortunately, our docket is to protect you as you play with your Ouija set," the agent continued.

"So, what do you recommend?" Chase asked.

"I sit watch at the house, bring two of you to set up our experiment, and Agent Sohn can dig through the town a bit," Jeffers suggested.

"Dr. Chase, why don't you come with me? You have a sort of celebrity status around here. I may be able to use that to my advantage," Agent Sohn declared.

"Sounds good. Wally, you know what to do?" Chase looked at his engineer, who looked a bit miffed that he wasn't the tag-a-long with the alluring agent.

"Of course. I'll run baselines, Tannen can reset the cameras, and we will do a daylight perimeter," Wally replied.

"Maybe we can debunk some of what happened last night in the remaining daylight," Tannen suggested.

Nodding, the professor, followed Danica Sohn towards the mayor's office.

"So," the FBI agent's tone was grave, "Have you seen anything like last night?"

Dr. Chase looked at Danica Sohn for a moment, "If you mean someone reacting wildly in the course of an investigation – yes. People get the willies all time, especially when they are not used to the situation. Now, that level of a reaction, from a trained agent – that is something of an extreme. Cardiac arrest from a healthy individual- absolutely not."

"What happened with Wally?"

Chase shook his head. "I am not sure. You've seen him. He's pretty unmoved by the creep factor. I have never seen him react the way he did last night. What it means, I don't know. I would guess a reaction to Agent Dunlap, perhaps seeing that and the agent nearly die, might have stripped away some of the protective shell."

"I can see that. Watching Agent Dunlap…that was scary stuff. Something you never want to see, never mind with a partner," Sohn nodded.

"What is your plan in town?"

"Courtesy call on the mayor; let him know we are going to be conducting some interviews. After that, start hitting up the natives."

Agent Jeffers sat a statue in the shotgun seat. With his aviator glasses on, he looked straight ahead at believed to be the most monotonous countryside he had ever seen. A strip of blacktop amidst a vast, endless sea of waving cornstalks. His brain ached for stoplights, buildings, trees…in the end; he decided he would have settled for a curve. He was even annoyed when Wally cursed that he had yet again failed to grab anything before leaving town.

Pulling into the lonely farm stand, even Special Agent Jeffers got out, happy for a change in scenery. Once more, they found the farmer snoozing under his hat. Jeffers looked at the paranormal pair.

"He's alive," Tannen assured him.

"Are you sure? Probably died of boredom," Jeffers said, surveying the area around the stand. Aside from the small white house behind the stand, he saw more of the endless sea of crops.

"I hear you. You fellas're back. Didn't get enough of Helberg yet?" the farmer laughed from behind his hat. Standing up, he stood beside the counter, "What for ya today?"

"I am starving. What have you to eat?" Wally asked, eyeing a package of flavored sunflower seeds.

"Some great corn chowder, the misses own recipe. Corn fritters, only take a few minutes to whip up..." the farmer started.

"Nothing we need to wait for," Jeffers snapped.

"Ha," the farmer scoffed, "Nothing but time around here, friend."

"Fine. I'll just take a sack of those sunflower seeds and another cup of your tea," Wally said.

"Different brew than yesterday if that's alright," the farmer responded.

Nodding, Wally dug out a handful of crumpled bills and handed it across the counter.

"I see you have water now. I'll grab a bottle," Tannen added.

The farmer grinned, "Got them just for you. Not sure why well water ain't good enough, but if you want to pay for it, well, figured I'm not gonna stop you."

"I'll have one of those too," Jeffers said, ignoring his soliloquy. "So, what's with the place, anyhow?"

"Told the folks yesterday, bad stuff there. Helberg was an ornery old coot. Even when he died, he screwed the town over. Could have sold his land to someone local, instead, signed it over to some corporate land trust from Chicago. They offered me the land for twice what they paid. I told 'em to stuff it. Only, Helberg had the best well around, perfect for irrigation. Wouldn't surprise me if his stinking old corpse wasn't still causing trouble. You're begging for it too if you ask me," the farmer rattled off in a surprise purge.

He eyed the group as they turned for their vehicle, "That ambulance last night for you? I ain't one to buy into a bunch of voodoo, but something there is not right. You be careful."

As Wally wheeled the van on the highway, Agent Jeffers slid his glasses down so that his eyes could be seen, "Charming."

Agent Sohn politely sipped at the lemonade placed in front of her. "So, Ms. White, what is your understanding of the events that have taken place here?"

The young woman looked at the agent and then rested her eyes on Ryder Chase. She took a moment to study him. His face was serious yet kind. His soft blue eyes were welcoming if a bit distant. Angela White thought the professor was even more attractive in person than on television. "It's that house. It's evil."

Sohn wrinkled her brows, a bit daunted by the young woman's distraction with the professor. "What do you mean the house? And how is it evil?"

"Something happened there. No one knows for sure what, but it wasn't good. After that, everyone who has ever been in it has had terrible things happen to them. The Helbergs weren't bad people, but they died unhappy. Their unhappiness affected that house," the young woman replied to the agent before redirecting her gaze to Chase. "You know how that can happen, don't you Ryder? Can I call you Ryder?"

"Uhh...sure. It is theorized that events can create an energy that is absorbed into places and things. Within that given theory, I suppose that is possible," Chase admitted. His face concerned, he asked, "What exactly happened?"

Angela White looked meek as she replied, "It happened about the time I was born, maybe a little before. Maggie Helberg, that was the daughter. She died. Some kind of an accident. That is when the Helbergs changed. Almost understandable, really."

"Almost," Sohn admitted coolly, "You say this happened *before* you were born?"

"Around that time," Angela confirmed.

Agent Sohn sat back and sighed. Her witness was not much of a witness.

"Have you had any experiences at the Helberg House?" Chase asked.

Angela's eyes brightened, and she clamped her hand down on Chase's, "Yes! Oh, Ryder, it was horrifying. Just recently, I was riding my bike…"

"Bike? Are you old enough to drive a car Ms. White?" Sohn broke in.

"Yes…I'm a junior in college, why?"

Chase waved her off, "Please continue."

"Well, I was riding my bike. It was a couple of months ago. It was like I heard a whisper. I first thought it was the wind. But the crops weren't very tall yet, and they were green. They aren't very noisy at that stage, just kind of a soft whoosh, not the crackle that this time of year sounds like. I didn't want to, but I stopped anyway. I swear it was coming from the house. It was little Maggie!" Angela White looked exasperated as she dropped the bombshell, a little disappointed as to how unmoved her two interviewers were, especially Ryder Chase.

"Could you make out any discernible words?" Dr. Chase finally asked, eliciting a warm sigh from the girl.

Angela sat up excitedly, "Well, I can't be sure, but it sounded like it said hellloooo!"

"Hello?" Sohn asked.

"Yes, I think."

"Could it have been 'help'?" Chase asked.

"Hmmm, didn't think about that. Could have I guess," Ms. White nodded happily. "Ryder, you are so good at what you do. Thank you for coming to our town to help us."

Chase accepted the sentiment graciously.

"Well, we have lots of vital witnesses to interview, so we should probably be going," Agent Sohn declared and rose from her seat.

"You have to go?" Angela said, disappointment dripping from her words. Bursting out of her chair, she streaked to a box next to a China hutch. Meeting the investigators in the hall, she produced a plastic bowl and handed it to Chase. "It's our newest collapsible model, seals tight for fridge and freezer," she declared.

Unceremoniously she thrust a spatula at Agent Sohn with a catalog. "If you book by the time you leave, I can set up a Facebook party for you."

The agent frowned at the catalog, "Thank you. I'll be in touch if I do."

As swiftly as she could, the agent moved to the door, holding it open for the professor. Unsure if he was just being cordial or in some unobvious way liking the attention he was receiving from the college student.

"Ryder, it was very nice to meet you," Angela said, her hand on the paranormal investigator's upper back.

"Goodbye, Ms. White, thank you for the information," Chase replied and walked past Agent Sohn, almost using her as a barrier from further flirting.

When the two were well out of earshot, Agent Sohn remarked, "Well, that was interesting. So, you what, have groupies?"

Chase looked at the agent, his brow wrinkled, "Groupies? I sometimes run into people that have seen my work. Not the best eyewitness, however."

Sohn nodded, "Kind of a waste of time."

"Not completely," Chase disagreed. His comment caused the agent to cock her head. "She gave us more insight on the girl who lived there. We need to find out what happened to her exactly."

"That, I think, will take sorting through the folklore to get to the facts," Sohn said.

"Who's next on our list?"

The agent scanned the sheet. "Elmore Grandly."

The home was on the outskirts of town, closest to the highway. Parking on the quiet street, they walked up a cement path. The walkway was cracked with sprouts of vegetation growing up through it. Two old vehicles sat idle next to the house; neither looked like they had been driven in years. The smell of must, rotting vinyl, and lubricate hung in the humid air. Chase found the aroma unusual, but not necessarily unpleasant. As they creaked up the steps, a new odor overtook them. This one Agent Sohn was unfortunately familiar.

Shooting an unsettling glance at the professor, she unholstered her sidearm, "You better wait here, Dr. Chase."

"Ryder," he mumbled but nodded that he understood. He watched as the agent pointer her weapon towards the ground and pushed through the screen door on the porch. Peering through the smudged windows of the front door, she released her left hand from the firearm and tried the door. Despite a protest from the hinges, it swung freely, and the agent disappeared inside.

NINE

The pungent odor was nearly unbearable, reminiscent of leftovers that had been left in the sun for days. The warm stale air and humidity only amplified the stench. Danica Sohn moved with caution, though she assumed that there was no need. Walking into the house, she worked from room to room. Searching for movement and signs of life first, then the floors and furniture. In the hall between the bedroom and bathroom, she found was she feared she would. The limp body of a man.

The man's skin was pasty and grey. The life and the color had fled him. Despite every neuron urging her not to, Agent Sohn knelt for a closer examination. The man's eyes were still open- vacant and grey. Turning away, Danica Sohn choked off the urge to vomit.

Returning to her review of the body, she did an obligatory check for a pulse. The lifeless skin brought back the impulse to purge. Confirming what she already knew, she declared the victim dead. Searching for identification, Agent Sohn smoothed her hand across the man's pockets. Feeling a wallet, she said, "Excuse me..." Flipping the wallet open and seeing the ID, "Yes...Mr. Grandly."

Performing a quick sweep of the rest of the house, the FBI Agent called in the deceased resident. Starting in the bedroom, Agent Sohn starting piecing together the scenario. Grandly was dressed for the day, but perhaps just so. Began feeling discomfort, moved from the bedroom into the hallway heading towards the bathroom and...

In her peripheral vision, Danica Sohn caught a shadow moving past the doorway near the living room. Carefully sliding the firearm out of its holster, her thumb found the safety. With careful footsteps, she crept towards the hallway. A creak on a floorboard in the living room heightened her wariness. With soft, controlled breaths, she inched forward. Watching her footsteps over the unfortunate Mr. Grandly, she was startled by a figure spinning into the hallway. Instinctively, she raised her Beretta and slid her finger onto the trigger.

Letting out a loud sigh, she thumbed the safety and put her gun away. "I thought I had told you to wait on the porch."

"It was taking a while, and I thought..."

Agent Sohn uncharacteristically snapped at the professor, "If we are going to work on this investigation together, I need you to follow my commands in a tactical situation. I'll follow your lead with ghost stuff, but I need you to do the same. That is how I can do my job and keep you alive, never mind preserve the sanctity of a forensics scene."

Chase looked down at being chastised, "I'm sorry, I wanted to make sure you were okay."

The agent instantly softened, "It's alright. As long as we are clear moving forward. Now, do not touch anything before we can properly establish the situation and get the body to the examiner. Agent Jeffers and Dunlap are on their way; they have remanded your team back to the hotel."

"I am glad to hear Agent Dunlap is feeling better," Chase replies and then suggested, "Why don't I try and locate the next witness."

Agent Sohn hesitated before relenting, "Sure. But if you see anything out of sorts, do not enter the location, call my cell, and we will meet you."

Nodding in understanding, Chase left the house. He moved quickly, eager to get himself into fresh air. Once back outside, he inhaled an enormous breath and another, expelling the stench of the house. Pulling out the sheet of paper with residents who had indicated insight into the Helberg house or the medical events.

The town was simple to navigate. A grid made up of only a handful of streets either direction, laid out in alphabetical order, allowed him to find the next witness quickly. Walking up the front steps, he found himself inexplicably moving in silence, cringing when the intermediate step emitted a loud groan. Pausing, he listened to see if the board had prompted an alarm. Shaking his unease out of his thoughts, he continued to the door and rapped softly on the wood frame.

After the last location, Chase was almost nervous when someone didn't instantly appear to greet him. After another tentative rap, a voice from inside the house called out, "I'm coming!"

In moments, an older man appeared in the doorway. He adjusted his John Deere cap and pushed on the door. "You're the fella from the Mayor's office."

"Yes sir, Dr. Ryder Chase," the professor held out his hand.

The man grasped the professor with a surprisingly firm grip, "A doctor, huh?"

"Not a medical one," Chase explained, "A Doctor of Psychology."

The man nodded, "A shrink. Come on in, just don't examine my head, even if there is something wrong, I don't really want to hear about it."

Inviting Chase into the living room with an extended arm, the man introduced himself, "I'm Jonah Gibbs. Please sit."

"You indicated that you might have some information on this case?" Chase asked.

The man looked hard at the professor, "You believe in all this stuff?"

"I do," Chase nodded, "Even though I have been working in this field for years, I am still chasing after that incontrovertible proof that I can use to show the rest of the world."

"Seen some stuff, eh?"

"Things most people wouldn't believe," Chase admitted.

"Doesn't spook you?"

Chase shrugged, "There are times I am unnerved, usually during evidence review, not often at the scene. Even so, I try and remember that they were people once. Good people, bad people, everyone in between."

"What about demons? They ain't people," Jonah Gibbs shared.

Ryder leaned in close, "Think there's a demon involved at Helberg?"

Gibbs stared long at Chase's eyes. "No. Least, I don't think so. Sadness, maybe a little madness."

"Why would you say that?"

"The girl. Helbergs were good people. Church every Sunday, shared their crops with those who struggled…real stand up family," Gibbs replied. "Then, Maggie died. They weren't right after that. Can't say I blame 'em. I probably wouldn't have either. They started keeping to themselves. Their crops were always the weakest yield, and one by one, they died unhappy."

"Sounds like a sad story," Chase conferred.

"Sad, alright. But they weren't done. Someone, maybe the whole family is still there. Their neighbors, you met them? Tom Brennan and I, we were asked to clean out the place and get it ready to sell for the state. I tell you what, we had the chills the whole time, like someone was watching us. Then the giggle. Tom and I both heard it. We couldn't get out of that place fast enough," Gibbs shivered.

"Can't say I blame you. Know what happened to the little girl? Why she died?" Chase asked.

Gibbs shook his head, "No more than what the papers said. An accident. A sad accident."

"Well, Mr. Gibbs, thank you for your hospitality and the information," Chase held his hand out for the farmer to shake.

Grasping the professor's hand tightly, Gibbs said, "I hope you find what you're looking for out here, Professor. Maybe little Maggie needs your help."

"We'll do what we can," Chase nodded.

As he left the house, bounding down the sagging steps, Chase let out a deep breath. This case, this town, was far more interesting than he had figured them to be. Deep in thought, he was startled by the voice calling to him from the street. "Dr. Chase...Ryder!" The professor found the scowling face of Danica Sohn staring at him as she tried to gain his attention.

"Agent Sohn..."

"I was beginning to worry about you. I had hoped you would have checked in," Danica snapped.

"I didn't realize," Chase began, "Jonah Gibbs, pleasant old man. Any more information from poor Mr. Grandly?"

"Cardiac arrest. Like the others. The only strange thing was his body temperature was a little warmer than it should have been for how long he had passed," Sohn shared as the professor climbed in the passenger seat.

"How atypical is that?" Chase asked.

"Relatively. We have seen it in a few cases in sudden death with athletes and rave party victims."

"Interesting," Chase said. "Not sure I would figure Grandly for a doping athlete."

Stifling a laugh, "Nor exactly rave material. Any ideas?"

Chase shrugged, "People react differently to fear. Some get cold shivers and turn pale. Others get flush. Could be an overstimulation of the adrenal gland, a chemical change in the body in response to fear, I don't know."

"Jeffers and Dunlap are headed out to the house now. Ready to head out there and meet up with them?"

"Night one was fascinating. Let's see what a second go has in store for us," Chase nodded.

TEN

The evening sky dazzled in streaks of pink over the Helberg House and surrounding acres of corn. Ryder Chase couldn't tell if it was beautiful or just made the place even more eerie. As Agent Sohn pulled the SUV in the driveway, Agent Dunlap was leaning against the open door of the paranormal team's van peering over the Don Tannen's shoulder.

"Reviewing last night again?" Chase asked as he strode up to the van.

The agent nodded, "I tell you, I saw something. I think it touched me, that's when you see the FLIR swing. Next thing you know, I'm face down in the hallway."

"Well, just to be safe, why don't we have you and Wally sit tonight out," Chase suggested.

"Oh, no. I'm fine," Wally snapped, indignant at the professor's recommendation.

Chase glanced at Tannen and back to Wally, "You sure?"

Wally just rolled his eyes and started stuffing his pockets with flashlights and recorders.

"Let's lock it down, and we'll let you guys do your thing," Agent Jeffers said. He and Agent Sohn went inside the building while Dunlap made a circuit of the exterior.

"He seems to be taking this a bit more seriously," Tannen noticed.

"I think after what happened with his agent last night, he doesn't have much choice but to. I don't want to ride you, but take it easy tonight," Chase demanded to his second investigator.

"I will," Wally grumbled. Slamming his ice tea down, he checked his equipment once more and hopped out of the van.

"Don, I'll have one of the agents spell you after a while, and you can join us," Chase said to the EMT.

Tannen forced a toothy smile, "Goody. This place is just so charming."

Seeing the agents reappear from the house, Chase looked at Wally, "Ready?"

Nodding, the investigators grabbed their gear and headed for the house.

"You're all set," Agent Sohn said.

"Thank you," Chase replied. "What's your protocol tonight?"

Jeffers stepped up, "We'll have one agent running perimeter all night, one tucked inside the entry and one by your man in the van."

"Perfect," Chase conceded. "Glad you guys are here."

"You're alone on that sentiment," Jeffers mumbled. "I pulled entry duty, so I might as well go in with you guys and lock the door behind us."

The three men made their way into the house as the other two agents went on to their duties.

With light fading outside, the interior of the building enveloped in darkness. The air was still stale. The heat from the day left the familiar oppressive, humid atmosphere from the evening before. The smells, the anticipation, the customary moans, and groans of an old home – they all added up to heightened senses. Chase was not surprised this environment sent people over the edge.

Agent Jeffers pulled an old folding chair out and leaned against the frame of the entry door. From that position, he had a view of the stairs, the foyer, and the main hallway leading to the kitchen.

"Where to boss?" Wally asked.

"Let's start where we left off last night. We can retrace Agent Dunlap's steps. Put the recorders and a handi-cam in the hall just outside of the bathroom."

Trudging up the stairs, they moved to where they found the agent slumped on the floor. Shining ultra-violet flashlights, they scanned the room. Wally switched on the FLIR camera and inch by inch panned from corner to corner while Chase watched the display on a handheld tablet. "Pretty quiet right now. Why don't we set an IR camera up in the hallway, and I'll sit in here by myself and run an EVP? Here, sit in the hall around the corner with the tablet. I'll take the FLIR just like Agent Dunlap last night," Chase, swapping for the camera.

Sitting on the floor, Chase switched on his voice recorder and set it down in front of him. Turning off his flashlight, he set the FLIR in a spot that would catch as much of the room as possible. "Is there anyone here with me? Can you show yourself to me the way you did Agent Dunlap last night? You won't frighten me. I'm sure you didn't mean to hurt the agent."

Chase waited several moments for replies. He knew that more often than not, you didn't hear anything during the session, but instead in review the next day. "Are you a Helberg? Do you have something to share? What happened to Maggie?"

For a moment, he thought he heard something. Faint, but audible. Almost like soft footsteps. "Maggie, is that you?"

"Ryder, did you just giggle?" Wally called from the hallway.

"Uhh, no."

"Thought I heard a giggle. Carry on!"

"Maggie, you seem like a sweet girl. Do you like to play? I brought a toy for you. A doll. Here…" Chase pulled a small doll he picked up from the general store in town and placed it on the floor next to the recorder. "It's just for you. You can play with it."

Chase waited for several minutes in silence. Straining his ears, he searched for some sign that the little Helberg girl was curious enough to show herself in the room.

"Can you give us any sign that you're here?" Chase asked.

Suddenly, a large thud shattered the quiet. In an instant, Chase and Wally had their flashlights on and convened in the hallway. "You heard that too," Wally confirmed.

Listening intently, they crept along the hall, towards the direction of the thud. When their beams broke the head of the stairs, they heard a voice.

"Sorry!" Agent Jeffers called, "Field stripping my firearm. The receiver slipped off my lap."

Chase and Wally looked at each other with disappointment. "Alright, let's leave the IR camera running on the doll and keep the voice recorder in place. We'll see if Maggie will show herself without us there," Chase proposed.

"Let's try the basement," Wally suggested, "We haven't spent too much time down there."

Shrugging, Chase followed his second investigator down the steps. As they passed through the kitchen, heading towards the basement, Wally froze, holding his hand out to stop Chase. "Did you hear that?"

"Hear what?" Chase whispered.

"A voice. I couldn't tell what it said. Maybe female, maybe young."

"Where'd it come from?" Chase asked.

"Dunno. It was like close but really soft," Wally replied.

Motionless, they waited and listened. Minutes ticked by. Occasionally they could hear Agent Jeffers wriggle in the chair at the front door. A discernible pop or crackle from the cooling wood of the old house constricting. No more voices.

"Let's move on," Wally whispered. Opening the door to the cellar, a blast of cooler, musty air hit them. Carefully, they descended the steps into the basement. Shining their lights around, the UV beams picked up traces of animal urine on the floor along the walls. A random assortment of left behind items gave the mind a host of places where things could be hiding behind.

"We'll relax if we give the room a thorough inspection before investigating. Otherwise, our eyes and ears will work overtime to fool us," Chase said. Flashlight in hand, he moved around the room. The FLIR in his hand, he had Wally sweep with the EMF detector.

"Getting anything?"

"Pretty clean on the EMF. How about you?" Wally asked.

"Warm spot down on the wall over there. Right where the concrete is crumbled. I bet a critter of some sort is living in the wall."

"No surprise. Anything else?"

Chase moved the camera around the room, meandering around each box or discarded tool. "No, we should be good. EVP?"

"Let's do it. I've got a recorder," Wally agreed. Finding a spot to settle, he began offering questions. "Anyone down here with us? We'd love to talk with you. Can you give us some sign that you're here?"

After each question, they allowed the requisite pause. They invited whatever was there to set off the light on the KII EMF detector. As their eyes adjusted to the pitch black, Chase could see how people could easily let their imaginations run away from them. Especially with random shapes throughout the room. Each seemed to move at one point or another.

Overall, their experience was without note in the basement until Chase noticed movement on the FLIR. Almost as though it was manifesting in midair, just behind Wally's head, a heat signature began to form. Hovering, the size of a basketball, it began to move. Left to right, it crossed behind the investigator before stopping. Almost seeming to be studying Wally, it seemed to turn in this direction.

"Uh, Wally," Chase whispered, "Just beyond your left ear, I have something!"

Wally swallowed, fumbling for the switch on his flashlight. Taking a breath, he switched it on in the direction according to Chase. With his movement and the sudden illumination, an ear-shattering scream filled the room. In the beam of his light, Wally faced two glowing eyes. As soon as they appeared, they vanished in a burst behind an old farm implement.

Chase, unable to contain himself, let out a roaring laugh.

"It's not funny. That thing could have killed me!" Wally cursed, "Where the hell'd it go?"

"I think it when behind that cultivator thingy, probably trying to get back to the hole in the wall," Chase reported.

"Damn," Wally sighed, "Freaking opossum…nearly wet myself!"

"The way it moved, I couldn't quite tell what it was until you hit it with the flashlight. If it makes you feel any better, pretty sure scared the heck out of it too," Chase laughed.

"Very funny. I think I'm done down here," Wally said in disgust.

"Alright, buddy. Let's take a break out at the van, get some fresh air," Chase suggested.

Turning off their equipment, they headed up the stairs to be blinded by the beam of a flashlight. The tip of Agent Jeffers' pistol peeked just below the light. "Everything alright down there? I heard some…banshee, I think."

"We're fine. Wally was visited by a curious opossum," Chase informed the agent.

"Great. Who knows what killer mold we're ingesting in this dump, it's infested with rabid rodents," Jeffers snapped as he holstered his weapon.

"Oh, I think we'll be okay. We were just going outside to grab some fresh air, why don't you come with us," Chase offered.

"Sounds good. I'll swap with Agent Sohn and let her pull sentry duty. Worse than a stakeout I had to man on a mob accountant," Jeffers groaned.

Out by the van, Tannen tossed Chase a water bottle. Wally shook his head at the offer. "How's it going in there?" the EMT asked.

"Wally made a new friend," Chase grinned and shared the story from the basement.

Adding the various voices they thought they heard; they quickly reviewed the footage from the FLIR and the recorder Wally carried.

Shaking his head, Tannen pulled off his headphones. "I can't find the giggle or the voice."

"Maybe the recorder in the bathroom picked it up," Chase said hopefully.

Pointing at the screen, Tannen said, "Oh, that must be your opossum!" On the monitor, a ball of heat took shape over Wally's left shoulder and moved across to his left. When the animal moved to look at the paranormal researcher, only for an instant did it take the shape of an opossum.

"Well, what's next?" Tannen asked, pulling the transfer cord from the FLIR camera.

"I would like to spend a little more time in the kitchen area. That is where so many reports have been made. We have pretty good coverage upstairs where Dunlap had his…uh, incident," Chase replied.

"I'd like to have my chance inside,'" Tannen said.

"I can man your equipment in the van," Agent Dunlap offered.

"Agent Sohn, that puts you in entry duty, and I'll take the perimeter sweeps," Agent Jeffers declared. "The three of you can have at it inside."

"Alright, let's go," Chase closed his water bottle.

Taking a final sip of his tea, Wally patted his gear to ensure all was in place and followed his team towards the house.

"What's the plan, chief?" Wally asked as he caught up.

"We have done most of the rooms. It seems we can chase noises all over the house. How about we all take a different leg of the stairs? That way, when we hear a sound, we can isolate it and have a better chance of running it down," Chase suggested.

"Sounds like a plan," Tannen nodded.

"I'll take high- between the second and third floor, Tannen, take the middle…" Wally directed.

"I've got the basement," Chase agreed.

"Have fun, boys," Agent Sohn said as she locked the front door and took her seat at her post.

One by one, the crew assembled in their positions. Tannen held the FLIR and switched on his voice recorder. Propping his elbows on the top step, he settled in and let his senses drink in the darkness.

A floor above, Wally leaned against the wall atop the stairwell. With an IR camera, he snapped pictures down the steps, and along both sides of the hallway. With each series of shots, he would review the photos on the small LCD screen of the camera.

Leaning against the doorjamb separating the kitchen from the cellar, Ryder Chase tuned his mind to covering both rooms. Using a tiny parabolic microphone, he scanned the area, holding the mic for several patient minutes before swinging it a new direction. The mix of smells, the stark contrast of the inky blackness of the basement versus the starlight fed kitchen put his senses on overload. Disciplining himself, he concentrated on one environment at a time.

As Chase waited, the parabolic in the direction of the kitchen, he could hear scratching. Softly at first and then with increased consistency. Carefully, he stood up and followed the sound. With one ear tucked in the headphones tethered to the recorder, the other left open to take in the natural sounds. Moving around the kitchen, he sourced the scratching in the area of the pantry.

He swore the door hadn't been completely latched the last time through. Pointing the parabolic directly at the door, the scratching was clear and persistent. Letting out a deep breath, he readied at the door. Gently placing his hand on the knob, he steadied himself. Tucking the recorder into his pocket, he freed his flashlight, thumbing the "on" button.

In one fluid motion, Ryder turned the handle and yanked it open while depressing the switch on the flashlight. Instinctively ducking as the pantry door swung wide, he lurched backward, startled by the eyes staring back at him.

All at once, Chase let out a sigh and cursed, watching the mouse scurry away from him and the light. "Really, Ryder," Chase scolded himself. He knew it was part of the course, seeing any movement in situations like that can cause the most seasoned ghost hunter to jump back. He was relieved no one was there to see it. Turning to return to his post at the steps, he froze as a floorboard let out a groan.

"Everything okay in there?" Danica Sohn asked as she swung a red light around the kitchen.

"Yes. The house, it seems, is host to a zoo full of nuisance animals. The second time something got me in the pantry," Chase admitted.

"Kind of explains at least some of the occurrences, doesn't it?" the agent asked.

"It does," Chase nodded, "Pretty common. Everything from creaky old wood, some places have old plumbing and electrical issues, others, like here, have pests that scurry and make noise."

"How can you tell them apart?"

"That's kind of the trick. If you can place a plausible solution, you throw it out. When you have unturned everything that makes sense, you end up with evidence. True evidence is rare," Chase said.

"Sounds frustrating," Sohn consoled.

Chase smiled, "Part of the allure, I think. The chase. The race to be the one to bring in truly incontrovertible evidence of the paranormal. It's tough. We have *really* good evidence. But it's never perfect. For those who did not experience it, there is always room for skepticism and doubt."

"Not a lot of confessions in your work," Sohn laughed softly.

"None that would be acceptable in a courtroom," Chase agreed.

Smiling at the professor, enjoying how his eyes light up when he talks about his craft, Agent Sohn relented, "I should get back to my post and let you get back to your work...and your furry little friends."

"Thanks," Chase scoffed. He paused as he watched the agent move down the hallway. Her fluid body glided silently down the hall as though she could have been an apparition herself. Chase let out a tense breath - a beautiful apparition.

Shaking his thoughts back to the task at hand, he retreated to his post at the top of the steps.

Don Tannen hated solitary "dark time" sessions. His safety-first mindset preferred to keep with the team's general guidance that investigators not at the base reviewing monitors had to stay in pairs. Not that this situation was all that disconcerting - they were all well within earshot and mere seconds from being able to respond to one another. Still, he had rather have remained together. From a purely scientific perspective, he rationalized, any personal experiences could be corroborated.

He decided he would sit back and listen, allowing the recorder to run without him asking questions. After all, the witness reports didn't have them calling out to a ghost, yet they seem to have gotten earfuls. That and he didn't want to go back and review hearing that someone was having a conversation right next to him without him knowing.

His eyes strained to adjust to the dark. He could barely make out the bannister next to him, nevermind anything else. Finding a little light spilling in from a window in the foyer, Tannen could watch the base of the stairs as a reference point. Even if he couldn't make out what a shape was, he could see if something crossed or passed through the lit area.

His senses on full alert, he allowed the house to offer up whatever it had planned for him.

ELEVEN

Agent Jeffers leaned back in the folding chair in front of the monitors. From his vantage, he could see a surprising amount of the old house. On the third floor, he could see Wally leaning against the wall, Tannen midway on the stairs and just see Chase's profile in the doorway leading to the basement. He was impressed with how seriously the paranormal team took their investigation and how surprisingly scientifically they approached the case. For a group who so badly *wanted* to find something, they went out of their way to prove themselves wrong.

Then again, the agent was equally impressed with how completely irrational they could be as well. Eyeing the fourth camera, so oddly placed staring all night at a bathroom. Sure, his own agent freaked out in there, but did they really expect to see anything magically manifest itself and smile for the camera? And that doll in the center of the frame, the whole thing was just a bit too far fetched and kind of creepy in a human disillusion sort of way.

He was about to move to the next screen when movement caught his eye. The doll in the center of the bathroom, which had been sitting upright the entire time he had been viewing the monitors, suddenly fell onto her side. Wrinkling his nose, he watched the screen intently, searching for shadows or other signs that someone was in there. Out of instinct, he almost grabbed his radio and reported it.

Cursing himself for falling into the group paranoia, he noticed the other screen on that floor. Don Tannen had moved from the center of the steps and leaned against the wall of the second-floor hallway. With no doubt in his mind, that the vibration of movement on those old creaky floors was more than enough to cause the toy to list. "Ridiculous, you put yourself in this silly situation, you'll start seeing and believing all kinds of crap," Jeffers muttered to himself.

Moving himself back in the chair, he removed himself from monitoring every detail to taking in the greater scene. Overwatch, to ensure the teams' safety. His intended role.

Wally sat with a slew of instruments in front of him. The KII meter with its band of colorful lights waiting to be brought to life, the voice recorder for the EVP, and his eye peering through at the LCD of the FLIR camera. He slowly brought the camera around the room. He never tired of seeing the rainbow of colors denoting heat variances that assembled detailed images. Wally focused, intent on trying to pick up any type of figure manifesting on the screen or temperature reading that was out of place.

It wasn't anything on the screen that first stole his attention. At first, he wasn't sure why, but he was compelled to stand up. Using the FLIR to see his path, he moved down the hall. Poking into one of the bedrooms, he scanned the room, drinking in every shape that appeared in the monitor. The room was clear.

Then he realized, one of the windows in the room had a section of glass missing from the panel grid. It was through this small hole his senses had beckoned him to investigate.

The now-familiar clatter of the cornstalks outside of the old farmhouse chimed as usual. Something broke their monotonous melody. Amidst the chatter was a crunching sound, like footfalls on a leaf-strewn path. Leaning to the open space in the window, Wally peered through.

At first, Wally's eyes did not discern anything out in the cornfield. Slowly, his eyes adjusted from the colorful

LCD screen to the darkness and the streaks of light that the moon afforded. The sea of waving cornstalks seemed endless, like an audience a million-strong marching in the field. For a moment, it reminded Wally of the scene he awoke to the night before, an army of ghouls marching through the farmland. Then movement caught his eye, a streak of cornstalks fell like spent dominoes. A meandering row began to lie down in a hasty path.

All at once, it stopped just outside of the window where Wally stood. Scarcely seventy feet away, a figure stood, halting the snaking trail of fallen stalks. It seemed to sense it was being watched. Cocking its head, it turned to face the farmhouse. Slowly raising its head to the third-floor window, it locked eyes with its observer.

Wally stood frozen, unable to believe what he was seeing- what was staring at him. A scarecrow with large eyes that glinted in the moonlight, a cold, unmoving glare targeted Wally. With a wicked grin, the scarecrow launched back into motion, streaking a path through the corn and way from the house.

Wally stood in place, trying to come to terms with what he had just seen. Looking down at the FLIR, he cursed to himself. He should have reacted and taken a picture with the thermal camera. Thrusting the camera in the direction the figure had retreated, Wally tried to find it again. The dark screen told him that there was nothing with warm blood to take a picture of.

Turning towards the hallway, Wally hesitated. He was afraid to share what he saw, yet hesitant to lose a possible piece of evidence. Shaking his head, still irritated for not getting a shot, he decided he needed to find the scarecrow.

Bolting out of the room and down the hall, Wally nearly slipped when he rounded to the corner of the stairs. Taking several steps with each bound, the paranormal investigator scurried down to the second floor. Navigating his way down the second flight of steps, he breezed past Tannen. Reaching the front door, Wally ignored Agent Sohn and blew through the front door. In a full sprint, Wally made for the cornfield.

Tannen heard the footsteps coming down from the third floor. Standing up, he started to ask his partner what was going on, but Wally didn't break stride. Confused and curious, the EMT followed him down the steps. At the front door, he looked at the agent who had gotten up out of her seat. With a mere shrug, Tannen could see that she didn't know what that was all about, either.

"What was that?" Chase's voice called as he scrambled down the hallway from the kitchen.

"Don't know. Suddenly Wally came bursting through like his butt was on fire and broke for the door," Tannen replied.

"Let's go find him," Chase said, switching on his flashlight.

Exiting the house, the three ran into Agent Dunlap, who rounded the corner. "Did I just see someone run out of the house?"

"Wally," Chase nodded, "We're going to find him now."

"Agent Dunlap, stand guard here at the door, I'll radio if I need you," Danica said as she followed the paranormal team toward the back of the house and the cornfield.

Ahead of them, they heard a violent crashing through the cornstalks. Seeing a trail blazed through the corn, they followed, with Agent Sohn taking the lead. With a small tactical flashlight positioned in tandem with her firearm, she played the beam along the narrow slice swathed through the cornfield.

Occasionally, the bounce of a flashlight beam bobbing above the corn in front of them told the trio they headed in the right direction. Before long, they caught up with the investigator. He was pacing around in a circle, playing his light at the wall of corn.

"It went through here, somewhere, I lost track through the stalks," Wally panted.

"*What* went through here?" Chase demanded.

"Scarecrow. The scarecrow," Wally replied, still studying the foliage for a distinct path.

"You saw a scarecrow...," Agent Sohn repeated.

"Yes. It was running through the field. It stopped and looked at me and then ran on," Wally nodded matter-of-factly, "I didn't think to get a picture until it was too late, so I decided to try and chase it down. I could see the path, and then I kind of lost. Each slight separation in the rows, all kind of looks the same."

Agent Sohn looked at Professor Chase and then at Tannen. Neither could offer anything more than a shrug.

Tannen stepped up, shining his flashlight at Wally. Noticing his friend looked flushed, he strode up to him and touched his screen. "You're burning up. You feeling okay?"

Befuddled and a bit irritated, Wally snapped, "I'm not hallucinating. I *saw* something, man!"

"I know, I believe you, but remember, this place tends to make people react to what they see," Tannen responded evenly. "Ryder and Agent Sohn can look around for clues and see if they can pick up the trail. I am going to look you over whether you want to or not."

The EMT slid his pack off his back and pulled out a few items to begin examining Wally.

Out of earshot, Agent Sohn and Chase splashed their flashlights around the field. "What the hell is going on around here, Dr. Chase?"

Ryder shook his head, "I don't know. That's twice for one of the calmest, most fearless investigators I know."

"I gotta tell you, I didn't see any converging path or swath built for two. All I see is one man's stampede through the corn," the agent said.

"I know, I can't disagree with you," Chase, shining his light around, hoping to find something that corroborated his investigator's story.

"Guys, he's running a fever, and his heart rate is through the roof again. I'm going to take him back to the van and get him calmed down," Tannen called.

"I'm fine!" Wally protested, wriggling away from the EMT.

"Wally, we're all packing it in for the night," Chase said.

"Since when Ryder? It's barely one in the morning," Wally retorted, shining his light on his watch.

"We have a ton of evidence already. We have no idea where the…the scarecrow might have gone. You know this place, you could travel a hundred miles in this cornfield."

"Fine, but I'm okay," Wally barked.

"I know, buddy, but we aren't going to take any chances on this one," Chase said firmly.

Conceding, Wally let Tannen escort him through the field and back to the van. There, the EMT performed a more detailed examination and ultimately ordered his friend to sit down with the heart monitor while Chase packed up the gear inside the house.

Inside, Agent Dunlap helped Chase gather gear. "What happened with your man Smyth?" the agent asked as he wound an extension cord.

"Thought he saw something, wanted to see if he could confirm it," Chase replied.

"What did he think he saw?" the agent asked.

"Uh…," Chase thought to respond cautiously, but realized the agents would all talk anyway, "Scarecrow."

"Yeah, so it's a cornfield, isn't that likely?"

"Maybe, unless they happen to be sprinting through it," Chase answered.

Dunlap stopped winding the cord for a moment, his face frozen in an incredulous stare. "Man, this place is nuts. And you guys do this all the time?"

Chase nodded but added, "But without the people in town keeling over and investigators needing medical treatment."

As they hauled the last piece of equipment out, Chase tuned back and peered into the inky blackness of the house. He wondered if they would uncover the dark secrets hiding in this strange place.

TWELVE

Chase woke up with the sun streaming through a slit in the curtains. He had barely recalled going to sleep. As soon as they got their gear locked up, he stood under a hot shower and hit his pillow.

Stretching, he yawned and saw his phone blinking. Seeing a message from Agent Sohn, he scrolled to it. The agents were meeting for breakfast in the town's diner. Glancing at the time the text was sent and then at the clock, he realized if he hurried, he might catch them. Forwarding the message to his team, he ran water though his hair and stuck his toothbrush in his mouth.

"A scarecrow. Running through the field. What's next, we're going to be chasing crop circles?" Jeffers scoffed from behind his cup of coffee. "I don't know what I have done wrong to get stuck on this ridiculous assignment. My career is obviously in the tank after this."

"*Something* is going on around here, Jeffers," Danica defended.

"What? This whole scared to death thing? Have you looked around at how these people eat?" Jeffers scanned the room. Pointing to various tables, he added, "A gallon of gravy...what is that, nine sausages? I don't even know what *that* is." A waitress whisked by with a plate of bratwurst patties steaming from the grill.

"Agent Jeffers, put your finger down. These are good people," Agent Sohn snapped.

"Maybe, I'm just saying it doesn't take the CDC to see that heart attack risk around here is not low," Jeffers replied.

"There's some truth to Jeffers' statement," Dr. Chase said, standing by the table. Behind him, Wally and Tannen pushed their way into the restaurant.

"Dr. Chase, good morning. I hope my text didn't wake you," Agent Sohn welcomed the professor and his team to squeeze around the table with them.

"The heritage of farming required a different diet than urban dwellers. Long days, often without breaking for lunch, mixed with serious physical labor, demanded hearty breakfasts. High protein, high carb, and fat were not a big concern for them. They would easily burn it off before they finally came back in for the day," Chase shared. Wrinkling his nose, he added, "Now, with the advent of modern machinery, farming has taken a different form. Still hard work, without a doubt, but different. Massive combines complete with air conditioning and even televisions in some cases. Their work is more like a long, grueling office day."

"Case closed, let's go home," Jeffers grinned.

"But…that's not what is causing the deaths here in Hope," Chase replied from behind his menu.

"What is?" Jeffers demanded.

"That is why we must stay, to find out," Chase said.

Throughout breakfast, the table received its share of looks from other diners. Chase wondered if it was because of the requests of egg white omelets and multi-grain toast or if people were curious about what their investigation was yielding. He didn't have to wait long to find out.

A man at the counter put down his paper and walked over to them. He seemed hesitant at first, but then halfway committed and closed the distance. "I'm sorry to disturb your breakfast," the man said, bowing his head slightly as he spoke, "I was hoping you had some word on what is going on around here."

Jeffers spoke up first, "I'm sorry, we are in the midst of a federal investigation, we aren't at liberty to disclose…"

"Grandly was a friend of mine. So was Sandquist. We all cared for Justin Marsh, just a teen, he was. I have a family. I want to know that I can keep them safe," the man shared.

"Mr.….," Agent Sohn began.

"Donnelly. Herman Donnelly."

"Mr. Donnelly, we are doing our best to come up with answers as soon as we can. This case has been pretty perplexing to this point. We are making progress, but nothing concrete. As soon as we do, as *soon* as we do, we will let you all know," Sohn said.

"Mr. Donnelly, I am sorry about your friends. We found Mr. Grandly yesterday. It seems, at least, that he may have suffered like the others. Can you tell us anything that might help? Was he ill?" Chase asked.

"Well, Horace was no longer an athlete anymore, that is clear. But he didn't have any conditions that I was aware of," Donnelly replied.

"Any idea what he had done the days before he…before we found him?" Chase asked.

Donnelly rubbed his stubbly chin, "He was in Cooperstown two days ago visiting his sister. She's in a care facility there. She broke her hip awhile back and has needed some help getting around. He was supposed to come back that night, as far as I know."

"Where's Cooperstown?" Agent Dunlap asked.

"'Bout a thirty-minute drive northwest of here."

"Past the Helberg House?" Dunlap pressed.

"Yeah, that's right," Donnelly nodded as the investigators shot each other glances.

When breakfast was over, and Jeffers successfully sidestepped more questioning residents, the team found Mayor Stenner in the Town Hall.

"How's the investigation? Sad to hear about Grandly, nice fellow, his sister is real broke up about it," Mayor Stenner said as the investigation team gathered in his office. "Sounds like you all have had your own run-ins yourselves. Everyone, okay?"

"We're all fine, thank you," Agent Dunlap replied.

"Good, good," the mayor said. "So, what have you come up with?"

"We have a lot of data collected, nothing concrete just yet," Chase admitted.

The mayor's face soured, "People around town are getting real nervous. Some have questioned if they need to take their families away, I gotta tell you, I'm not sure that's not such a bad idea. Myself, I don't drive past Helberg anymore. I'll take the loop around Highway 38 if I go north. Adds an extra twenty or so each direction, but every bit worth it, I'd say."

"You say people are thinking about leaving. There anyone who would benefit from having the town cleared out or thinned down?" Agent Jeffers asked.

The mayor cast a puzzled look, "What do you mean?"

"Like a business that's been poking around, digging for shale, anything like that?" the agent continued.

"Well, if they did, we'd probably welcome them, but no. A geological crew came through a few years back and did some tests and whatnot. We weren't one of the lucky ones," Mayor Stenner replied. "What are you getting at?"

Jeffers looked at Stenner serious for a moment. "Trying to figure out if there was any reason to drive your town out of existence."

"Is that what you think is going on?"

"I don't know. It is a theory that could explain the events," the agent shrugged.

Looking at the paranormal researchers, Mayor Stenner asked, "You don't believe it's Helberg?"

Wally started to speak, but Chase realized the sensitivity needed with the response, "We have more investigating to do. I am not prepared to declare anything paranormal or not, but there has been no shortage of difficult to explain activity. I like Agent Jeffers' approach of looking for other possible explanations."

"I see," the mayor nodded. "So, what's next?"

"Well, to further rule out any human-caused explanations, we need to track down the history of the Helberg's living here. Understand the leases and ownership of the land, that sort of thing," Chase explained.

"Any issues with squatters?" Jeffers asked.

The mayor looked at the agent, "You drove here. You can go a hundred miles and not see much but fields of the farmers' handiwork. Not much foot traffic from town to town out here, Agent Jeffers."

"I suppose not," the agent muttered

"Abigail, the girl you met when you first came to town, she also manages the city records. She can go over all that for you," the mayor offered.

The team thanked the mayor and huddled in the hallway.

Agent Dunlap clapped his hand together, "What's the plan?"

"Let's divide and conquer again. I'd like Tannen to stay in town, meet with Abigail and uncover anything on the land or the family, especially the Maggie, the little girl," Chase said, "I'd like to do a daytime investigation of the house and the surrounding area."

"Agent Sohn, how about you stay and see what you can find with Tannen, and we'll escort Dr. Chase back to the property," Agent Jeffers decided.

Nodding, Danica followed Don Tannen to track down the mayor's assistant.

They didn't have to go far, as the woman in her late twenties was peering around the corner behind a ficus tree. Startled, she smiled, "Very dry. I think this one needs watering!"

"Impressive, you have such interest in the office plants among all of your other duties," Danica quipped.

"Well, yes, Mayor Stenner always says he couldn't run Town Hall without me, but I think he is just being kind."

The agent and Don Tannen exchanged glances. "I'm sure you're too humble. In fact, the mayor was just informing us that you are in charge of the town records as well."

The assistant beamed, "Yes! I take great pride in preserving our town's history. Not much happens around here without me knowing about it."

Agent Sohn choked back a laugh, "I'm sure."

"Abigail," Tannen took over, "What can you tell us about poor Maggie?"

"Oh, *that* story. I was just a bee in Mama's bonnet. Such a tragedy. Really changed the town that day."

"How so?" Tannen raised his brows.

"The mood of the town wasn't the same. The Helbergs had the largest farm. They were the wealthiest family in the county, but they were also very generous. They were the core of our community. When poor Maggie died, their hearts were just broken, and they retreated from their friends and Hope. Some of the townspeople didn't realize that they had come to depend on the Helberg's generosity a bit too much. Sadly, some of them took offense to the family's retraction," Abigail informed the investigators.

"Can you dig up a copy of Maggie's death certificate? If there was a coroner's report, news story, whatever you can find," Agent Sohn requested. "Don, maybe with your medical training, you can review them."

Tannen nodded, "I'll take a look into the deaths recently, too. If you can use your credentials to get them turned over, at least."

"I will," Sohn agreed. "While you do that, I have my own hunch to play."

To all of the men, arriving at the Helberg House was a little less stressful in the daytime. At night, the entire backdrop shrouded in such absolute darkness. By day, the waving field of cornstalks adds a visible barrier, but not an imposing one. Instead, as the breeze blew over the tops of the tall plants, it felt more like pulling alongside a green seashore. The warm breeze carried with it a medley of scents, most pleasant – fertile earth, vegetables trying their best to grow in the heat.

Chase stood outside the van and stared at the field. All night, he had wondered what the seasoned forensic scientist had seen the night before. Patting his pocket to ensure his flashlight was in place, he immediately headed for the house.

"I want to check out the field," Wally declared. "I can't be sure what I saw last night, but I sure as heck want to find out."

"I know, I do too. But do not go into that cornfield, not just yet," Chase cautioned. "Get whatever gear you want out. I'll be right back."

Jeffers glanced at Agent Dunlap and ordered, "Stay here with Smyth. I'll head in with Dr. Chase."

The lead agent had to jog to catch up with Chase. "Weren't you wanting to check out the field?"

"Yes, we're going to," Chase acknowledged, pushing his way through the door. Making a beeline for the stairs, the professor glided up the steps.

Special Agent Jeffers suddenly nodded to himself, "Going to a higher advantage, good move professor."

As the pair reached the third floor, Chase counted the rooms until he got to the one Wally had noted where he looked out of the window the evening before. Shining his flashlight, he could see the dust obviously more disturbed by one sill versus the others. "This must be the one."

Scanning the site from the window, using the missing panel to get a view unobscured from years of dust. "Well, I'll be…"

Agent Jeffers muscled in next to him, peering down on the cornfield. Shaking his head, he could see what Chase was looking at. A thin trail of broken down stalks snaked its way from left to right, streaking across the backside of the Helberg House. On the far-right edge, he could just see where the search party went in and joined with the trail until disappearing from view.

"Look there," the agent noticed, "Almost directly in front of our window, the thin path bows slightly wider."

"Wally said whatever it was stopped and looked up at him," Chase said.

"Stopping and turning, especially in the dark, could cause you to knock a few extra stalks in this direction," Jeffers nodded.

The two studied the field for several minutes, trying to identify some sort of landmarks to note in the monotonous rows of corn. Jeffers turned to Chase, "Professor, ghosts typically lay down trails in their path, or are you going to suggest something like crop circles now?"

"There have been cases of the paranormal affecting their environment just as a person would, but it wouldn't be the most common case. Crop circles, no."

"Let's go down there. Maybe we can find some footprints or something. Finally prove there is human involvement going on. Probably just some kook in town playing a joke or something," Jeffers suggested.

"And causing otherwise healthy people to have heart attacks?"

"If a ghost could scare someone, couldn't a person?" the agent returned.

Chase studied the agent and conceded, "Yes. I suppose they could."

Following the agent, Chase made his way down the first floor and out to the van.

"Well, you're not crazy, Wally, at least not completely," Chase announced. "There is a definite trail cutting through the field."

"But no flaming-eyed scarecrows," Special Agent Jeffers admitted.

"I told you something was out there!" Wally scoffed.

"Now to find out what," Jeffers declared. "Mr. Smyth, head up to the third-floor window, take your radio with you, and a pair of binoculars if you have them."

"I have a range finder with a telescopic feature," Wally said, reaching into the van.

"Perfect. Lock up the truck and have Agent Dunlap escort you into the house, Professor Chase and I will head out to the field," Jeffers said, sliding his sunglasses out of his jacket pocket and placing them on the bridge of his nose. Instinctively, he patted his firearm and motioned for Dr. Chase to follow him.

Stopping where they entered the field the evening prior, Jeffers spoke into the radio, "Are you in position?"

"Almost, just rounding the stairwell onto the third floor," Agent Dunlap's voice crackled back.

"Let me know when in position," Jeffers responded.

A few moments ticked by before the junior agent's voice came back over the radio, "All set, Smyth is adjusting the range finder. The path is pretty distinct. Why don't you start forward, straight from your position about twelve yards?"

Moving carefully not to disturb any additional stalks of corn, Jeffers and Chase found the point where the two trails intersect. "Perfect!" Dunlap's voice sounded. "Now, to retrace the assailant's trail, move north directly from your spot on the trail."

Jeffers studied the crude, very thin swath of stalks that had been leveled. Ideally, he wanted to find footprints. Identify a modern pair of boots and put to rest, at least this part of the mystery, as supernatural. To his dismay, the corn itself, obscured the soil underneath. "Your ghost, it would appear, wanted to cover its tracks. Stepping clearly on the stalks."

"That explains the definitive path," nodded Chase.

"Let's move on," Jeffers declared. Into the radio, he said, "There's no place for prints along the path. Let us know when we have reached the spot just outside your window."

After a brief pause, Dunlap responded, "I got it. It looks like a spot where the maker of the prints stopped, probably stepped a bit off-trail. Your best shot at finding a track."

Maintaining their care, Jeffers and Chase moved steadily towards the breach in the trail. "Almost there," the radio called.

Jeffers motioned for Chase to stop behind him. Bending down, the agent inspected the ground. Hoping to find a break in the vegetation where he could see clear to the ground, he shook his head in disgust. "It's like they knew what they were doing," Jeffers muttered.

"Who is so careful that they don't misplace a step on a cornstalk in the middle of a field? I would find it the opposite. Generally, not stepping on a stalk, only occasionally misstepping and knocking into one by accident," Chase said, furrowing his brow.

"Someone who didn't want to be tracked," the agent replied.

"Let's see if we can find where the trail came from," Chase suggested.

The agent nodded, "Trail had to start somewhere. Maybe they weren't so careful leading into it." For a moment, the agent cocked his head at the professor, "You know, if you weren't into comic book stuff, I'd say you would make a pretty good investigator."

"I *am* an investigator, Special Agent Jeffers," Chase quipped back.

Ignoring the professor, Jeffers pressed on. Into the radio, he stated where they were heading, "While we head to the start of the trail, see if you two can find a high spot where you can identify where we lost the trail last night."

Step by step, Chase and Jeffers scanned the ground, searching for a spot where a shoeprint might have slipped through the stalk, but each step appeared to have fallen deftly on the corn. When they reached the road, they were even more stymied. The path vanished with the last stalk. It was if whoever had come through floated from the road to the field.

"Any ideas?" Jeffers asked, rubbing his eyes.

"I don't. At least none you would want to hear. It's strange, almost as if something didn't want to leave tracks," Chase bent down to the spot where the line through the corn began. The ground was clear of prints. "Hang on," the professor said, studying the dirt, "There is a section that doesn't match the rest."

Pointing the professor carefully made a wide circle around the entrance to the path. "It's almost as if it has been swept. Chase looked around. Spying a completely detached stalk at the start of the path, he announced, "There. Right at the head of the path, that stalk could have been used to sweep the tracks. But why?"

"Because there is a person who is pretending to be a ghost," the FBI agent declared flatly.

"Or at least a scarecrow," Chase corrected.

"Have you noticed there aren't any scarecrows around her?" Jeffers asked.

"I noticed," Chase confirmed.

Through his dark glasses, Jeffers stared into the distant cornfield, retracing the steps of the path. "So, where does this path go?"

Agent Dunlap and Wally Smyth moved to the room furthest to the southern wall of the house. Craning their necks, they tried to follow the path past the point that failed the group the night before. Wally, in particular, was focused on finding the end. He was irritated that he had been made to look foolish twice on this investigation.

The closed window refused to allow them enough of a view to see where the path led. Banging on the pane, they tried to pry the window open. Years of humidity, dirt, and seeping paint worked against them. Dunlap athletic and Wally big and robust, their efforts yielded little.

"Let's try to get a vantage outside," Dunlap suggested.

Without a better idea, Wally nodded. Descending the stairs, they burst through the front door. Confronted with the bright sunlight, they winced, putting a hand above their brows. Knowing Jeffers and Chase were closing in on the intersection, they searched desperately for a way to get an advantage on the site.

"The van!" Agent Dunlap nodded his head toward the vehicle.

Nodding, Wally raced to the driver's seat with keys in hand. Starting the vehicle, Wally maneuvered the van close to the edge of the field. Putting his foot on the passenger tire, Agent Dunlap leaped up on the hood and scrambled to the roof of the van. Lining up his sights, he scoured the area, looking for a clear trail. The cornstalks became increasingly sparse in that area, and it was more difficult to discern a definitive path.

"Maybe there…maybe there….," the junior agent swung the range finder around in an arc but really couldn't determine any particular trail through the field. The crackle over the radio told him that Special Agent-in-Charge Jeffers and the professor were at the intersection. He could see Chase's head stick up over the tall corn.

"What do you have for us, Dunlap?"

"I really can't tell. There are gaps in the rows there, but none that definitively separate from another," Dunlap admitted.

After a sigh, Jeffers relented, "We'll see what we can find from here."

In the field, Chase surveyed the ground. The area littered with prints, but any one of them could have been their own from the night before.

"Make concentric circles away from the middle," Jeffers suggested, pushing away from the intersection.

On the other side, Chase followed suit. Moving away from the center, he scanned the ground looking for prints that seemed different than the rest. When he completed his ring, he came face to face with Agent Jeffers. "Nothing?"

The agent shook his head. "Either someone is strangely adept at walking on cornstalks, or maybe you guys are right, there is a ghost out here in nowhereland."

"Well, who might be used to moving about the corn and lives say...*that* direction?" Chase pointed south through the sea of corn.

"The farmer, the one with the iced tea and stuff!" Jeffers snapped his fingers.

"And isn't he the one who leased the land?" Chase asked.

"Yes. He also seemed a bit disgruntled with the Helberg's for some reason," Jeffers added.

"Should we pay him a visit?" Chase asked.

Jeffers answered in his direct movement through the maze of corn and back towards the van.

THIRTEEN

When the team pulled up to the farmer's stand, the man was nowhere to be seen. Jeffers strode up to the porch of the old farmhouse. Rapping his knuckles on the screen door, he waited impatiently for a response. "Mr. ...," Jeffers scowled and asked the group, "What's his name?"

"Stilton," Agent Dunlap replied.

"Stilton!" the lead agent called out.

They all listened intently for footsteps on the old wood floors. None came. Instead, they were surprised by a voice from behind them. "Can I help you?"

The team whirled to see Stilton stride silently out of the cornfield. Jeffers hand instinctively fell to his holster.

Wally exclaimed, "He's a freaking corn ninja!"

"Can't exactly make a living if you don't learn not to trample the crop," Stilton said and then eyed the group suspiciously, "Speaking of, I've been noticing all kinds of ruckus through the field near Helberg. That you?"

"We did follow a...," Wally began before Jeffers swatted his arm.

"Follow a what?" Stilton asked excitedly.

"A lead. We needed a better vantage of the house. Sorry if we disturbed your corn," Jeffers quickly replied.

"No worries, agent. Sooner you clear up the matter of what is going on out there, sooner we can all relax and go about our lives."

"I appreciate that. We couldn't help but to notice tracks out there that seemed to lead right towards your farm," Jeffers declared and then leaning over to where Stilton was standing, inspected the ground. Flipping through photos from the field he had downloaded onto his phone, held an image up to the farmer. "It would appear that your shoe pattern matches those out behind Helberg."

Stilton scratched his head. "Ain't that a pickle? You found my footprints out in my field. Yep, that's a puzzler."

The farmer's glib nature was more of humored logic than defiance to the FBI agent's questioning. The man's affect gave Jeffers pause. Scowling, the agent rubbed his chin. "So, you are saying you aren't playing games out there? Either for some sick joke or hoping to make some kind of statement about Helberg?"

"I love a joke as much as the next guy, but I am up before dawn tending to my farm, I can tell you, no silly joke is worth loss of sleep for me," Stilton responded, "As for Helberg, well, I'd just as soon that damned place burn to the ground and put to rest like the family. But I don't need to stomp around in my field to share that. I'd just tell you!"

Chase stepped forward slightly, "Mr. Stilton. Have you noticed anyone near the house or your field?"

"Well, other than you folks, can't say as though I have," Stilton replied. Then he added, "Off the highway up past Helberg; I had noticed someone had pulled off the road, looks like they spun the tires a bit as they pulled back out. Figured kids or something. I'll occasionally find a tossed beer can or something along the road. Other than that, nothing out of sorts. Say, what is that all about, anyway?"

"Nothing," Jeffers replied. "Probably normal for people to see all kinds of things that are nothing more than the wind blowing through the corn."

"Saw something, did you?" Stilton grinned. Seeing Agent Dunlap yawn, he added, "I got something for you. My latest batch, gotta little kick to it. I like to add a spoonful of my own honey to it, whoo it's good. On the house for you boys today."

With the heat of the day already weighing on them, the team nodded.

"You make your own honey, huh?" Wally asked.

"The best," Stilton nodded. "Good to have bees around a farm. They were the original farmers, you know."

"I suppose so," Wally replied, accepting his cup of tea. Spooning an oozing helping of honey into his cup, he watched it seep to the bottom.

"Gonna be hot today!" the farmer declared to no one as he handed out the last cup.

The crew thanked him and returned to the van.

"What do you think?" Dunlap asked.

"Something's not right about that guy," Jeffers said.

"Maybe, but that doesn't make him some ingenious saboteur," Chase shrugged.

"He knows this area better than anyone. He slips in and out undetected as he pleases. Heck, he could be watching us the whole time, and we'd never know it," Jeffers declared, "And you heard him. He'd like to see the place burned to the ground."

"I don't know. He's a little squirrely to be sure, but he doesn't seem like a mastermind that can manipulate people's minds," Chase sounded doubtful.

"Just the same, we need to keep an eye on him. Someone is doing all of this, and I am sure as hell not ready to join your group's fantasy Professor Chase," Jeffers said.

"So, who left the tire marks?" Dunlap asked.

"Could've been Stilton himself. Whoever it was new were chasing after them. If Stilton knew, acknowledging that sort of thing happens all the time is a great way to get us off track," Jeffers replied. Pulling the van back in front of the Helberg house, he gulped his tea down and screwed his face, "How can you guys stand this stuff?"

"Why don't you guys run perimeter from the top floor of the house? We can lock the van down, and Wally and I can investigate a few more things," Chase suggested.

"Keep an eye for our farmer friend," commanded Jeffers to the junior agent.

Wally nodded to Chase, "Let's do an EMF panel of any of the discarded items that have been left behind. Sometimes energy can be trapped with an object."

"Sounds good, while we're at it, we can look for any hiding spots- loose boards, little nooks something may have been left behind." Gathering gear Chase locked down the van and headed for the house. Wiping the sweat off of his forehead, he marched up the porch and into the house.

Making a beeline for the basement, Chase and Wally blanketed the damp room, scanning every article they could find. Rusted farm equipment was once more carefully inspected. Mounting the FLIR camera to capture any changes in heat they did not catch, the pair carefully flowed their EMF detectors over every item they could find. Some of the old pieces looked promising as they were positively sinister. From old scythes to random parts from a derelict oil heater, there was plenty of history under the rust.

Exhaustive in their inventory, Chase shook his head, "Absolutely nothing."

Wally called from across the room, "Me neither."

"Let's see if we can find what secrets this place is hiding," Chase suggested.

Playing his flashlight across each corner of the room, from the ceiling to the floor, the professor looked for anything that could be moved or opened. Using an Ultraviolet light, Wally did the same. "Watch out for vermin!" he chirped.

"Trust me, I am," Chase grumbled.

Finding a loose brick, Chase tried prying it. Using his hotel key, he tried to scrape along the mortar, unsure if it was still in place or years of dust and dirt had resealed it. Eventually, he was able to work the brick free. As he pulled it, a sea of silverfish spilled out of the opening it revealed. Instinctively jumping back, he dropped the brick and allowed the scurrying creatures to evacuate and find new hiding places among the junk and cracks in the walls. Reluctantly, he shone his light through the hole. The light revealed very little space behind where the brick had been and the exterior wall. Satisfied the protruding masonry was just affected by age and not a secret cache, he backed off and continued his scan of the area.

"Hey, Ryder!" Wally shouted from the far end of the basement. "I may have something! Come look at this!"

Chase found his tech studying a pile of bricks. Behind the rubble looked like a crude trap door. Finding a discarded tool that looked sturdy enough, he began sweeping blocks out of the way. After a few hearty swipes, the door was free enough to open.

"Probably a hatch for firewood. It leads to outside. The bricks probably formed a bin," Wally suggested.

Nodding Chase added, "Exterior wall, it should line up just about ground level. Let's take a peek."

Using the same tool, Wally pried the door open. As it swung away from the wall, a dark form fell towards them. Both men jumped back with Wally aiming the hand tool menacingly.

Chase directed his flashlight beam at the object. Furry and roughly the size of a cat, he hesitated to look any closer at the matted lump of fur. Irreverently, Wally prodded the carcass. Curiously, he gave it another couple of pokes and then bent over, snatching it from the rubble heap. Looking on in horror, Chase was relieved to hear him declare, "Teddy bear!"

Excitedly, Chase thrust his KII meter at the gnarly stuffed animal, jabbing at the button with his thumb. Instantly the lights flashed, making the investigators' hearts leap. Using a more scientifically calibrated EMF detector, he looked confused. At the same time, the KII lights dissipated.

The pair looked at each other. Chase shrugged, "KII anomaly?"

Disappointingly, the tech nodded, "That's the only we can rule it. Was it a blip from your movement, or was something there that went away? No way to know."

"Well, the bear is an interesting find anyway," Chased suggested.

"Think it belonged to the Helberg girl?" Wally asked, inspecting the bear. It was missing an eye, and one of its arms was literally hanging by a thread. Its dingy fur was grey and matted.

"Maybe...maybe."

Agent Sohn found Dan Tannen flipping through photocopies of Maggie Helberg's medical charts. "Find anything good?"

Tannen spun and studied the agent for a moment before answering. "Sad, really," he replied quietly.

"She was just a little girl. The injuries in the coroner's report were consistent with the accounts. She died from a contusion to her head. It likely caused inflammation in the brain, which they probably were not adept at identifying back then."

"Unfortunate, but we already knew that," Sohn remarked.

"Yes, but it is worse. She did not die immediately from the injury. It would have taken at least an hour or two for her brain to have swelled to the point that it would be fatal. The report showed that she died before the doctor got to the house," Tannen said solemnly.

Danica sighed, "She suffered before passing, the poor little thing."

Tannen nodded, "It seems like it."

"So, either her injury was ignored, they didn't know what to do, or couldn't find the doctor,'" Danica mused.

"That's about the long and short of it," Tannen nodded. "How about yourself?"

"Well, we knew that kooky farmer Stilton had a bit of a spat with the Helbergs. It turns out it was a long-standing feud. They had once shared the land, split the work, split the profits. About the time of Maggie's death, Helberg reneged. He booted Stilton off of his portion. Likely it cut Stilton's profit from farming in half. A pretty big deal," Agent Sohn shared.

"Sounds like motive for mischief."

"Perhaps...," Danica started and then paused as she turned to watch two fire trucks roar out of the station.

As they watched the engines drive away, they heard someone from across the street call to their friend, "Helberg House. Just got a fire called in!"

The agent on the third floor of the Helberg House paced back in forth. With each pass, they spied out of the windows canvassing the front and as much of the cornfield as possible. With several of the windows open, they hoped the breeze would be cool, but it just blew with it more hot air. Dunlap swirled his cup of tea, hoping there was still some liquid in it. Even unflappable Jeffers loosened his tie and freed a button on his collar.

"It's burning up in here!" Dunlap complained.

"What did you say?" Jeffers asked, "Do you smell smoke?"

Dunlap looked at his superior and inhaled. Shrugging, he said, "It's hard to tell. This place smells weird anyway. Is that smoke or dust?" The air filled with a warm swirling cloud. The agent felt his pulse quicken, and his skin flush.

"We better warn the geeks and check it out," Jeffers said.

The agents ran down the stairs, meeting up with the paranormal team in the kitchen as they were ascending the cellar steps. "Do you guys smell anything?" Jeffers asked.

"Like what?" Chase frowned.

"Something burning?"

Chase and Wally both took in big breaths. "I can't tell."

"We thought we saw smoke upstairs, but it as tough to tell with all the dust," Tannen reported.

The team slowly moved through the first floor, sniffing the air. As they made their rounds, a gust of warm wind blew into the room, with it, a thick cloud. "Fire! Let's get out of here!" Jeffers called, instantly grabbing his cellphone out of his pocket. The four men burst through the front door and out in front of the house as the FBI agent called in the fire.

"It was so hot in there!" Agent Dunlap panted.

"It was hard to breathe," Wally gasped.

Chase was desperately searching the house for flames, his heart racing. When Jeffers finished the call, he too scoured the exterior of the building.

"I don't see any flames," Jeffers reported.

"Must be in the walls!" suggested Chase

Jeffers nodded, "Must be. I couldn't get out of there fast enough!" The agent removed his jacket and released another button on his shirt, completely undoing his tie.

In minutes, the first fire truck arrived, and three men rushed up to the men. "The fire is in the walls, we think!" Jeffers reported.

"Which floor?" one the firemen asked as he flipped his mask down.

Jeffers scrunched his face, "Second?"

"I thought it was the first," Chase shared.

The fireman didn't wait for further debate as he turned on his flashlight and entered the building while the other two men were preparing the hoses and pumps. A second engine arrived, followed by the SUV with Tannen and Agent Sohn.

Wally had turned on the FLIR camera and started combing the exterior walls. As the second engine crew readied to go into the house and the hoses were prepped, Sohn and Tannen had joined the group.

"See anything?" Tannen asked Wally.

"Not yet, nothing is standing out on the FLIR," the tech reported as he continued his scan.

The first fireman burst through the front door. Flipping up his mask, he looked confused. "Where did you say the fire was?"

A medley of answers volleyed and ultimately met with a shrug. "Alright, boys, search the building. Go in pairs and use your oxygen," the man commanded and returned to the building.

The investigation team looked on for fifteen minutes expecting the activity to pick up or start seeing smoke, and flames burst through the windows. After a thorough inspection, the firefighters all returned to the front lawn, their helmets in their hands. The one who appeared to be in charge walked up to Special Agent Jeffers. "You're the one who called it in, right?"

"Yeah, that was me."

"You sure there was a fire?"

Jeffers looked incredulous, "Of course. Why would I call it in otherwise? These guys know it too" Waving his arm at Dunlap, Chase, and Wally, they joined him in his defense.

"You could smell it."

"I saw smoke," Wally nodded.

"I don't know what to tell you," the fireman said, "Nothing is going on in there. My men searched every floor, scanned every wall with one of them things." He pointed to Wally's FLIR.

"Nothing?" Jeffers pressed.

"Nothing," the fireman confirmed and motioned for his crew to pack up.

"What the heck happened here?" Agent Sohn asked.

Chase, who had been biting his lip. "Tannen, quickly run vitals on all of us."

The EMT shrugged but started checking pulse rates. "Your skin is really hot. I know it's a hot day, but this is unusual. Your heart rate is up, too."

One by one, he gave similar assessments to the other three who had been investigating the house.

"Group delusion," Chase said quietly.

"What?" Jeffers snapped.

"Elevated blood pressure, spiking body temperature, paranoia and hallucination or at least some form of visual matrixing. We all shared it. How did it start?" Chase asked.

"Right about the time I noticed how hot it was, Jeffers asked if I smelled something," Dunlap reported.

"Even the breeze is hot. Couldn't be sure, but it looked like smoke was rising from the floor below," Jeffers added.

"You guys came downstairs, told us what you thought, and then we were all spun to a frenzy, driven to leave the house. We had a shared delusional experience," Chase said.

"Great. Now I'm going as batty as you guys," Jeffers sighed in disgust.

"We influenced each other. A suggestion fed us to the point where we truly thought the house was on fire," Chase explained.

Tannen snapped his fingers, "I said I was burning up. That was right before Jeffers thought he smelled smoke."

"There you go. One suggestion snowballed. But why?" Chase continued.

"'Cause this place is cursed," Tannen offered.

"There's no such thing as curses. Or ghosts or walking scarecrows," Jeffers snapped, "Probably something in the water."

Chase shrugged, "Could be. I know some basic medical conditions were originally tested, but we could run a more complete panel."

Jeffers looked at the professor, surprised his remark met with positive feedback. "All right. Maybe we can finally make some sense of this."

FOURTEEN

Dr. Chase waited inside the reception foyer of Town Hall. Abigail stood behind the counter, a hollow smile washed over her face. Her blue eyes peered over her glasses as she measured the professor patiently.

Chase shifted a bit, uncomfortable under the weight of the receptionist's stare.

"I watched your show," Abigail finally spoke, "The one on that science channel. You were in some old asylum, very creepy."

Ryder smiled, "That one was in Pennsylvania. I have to admit, that *was* a very creepy place."

"How do you do it? I'd have been scared out of my wits."

Ryder shrugged, "The murder rate in haunted places is pretty low. I do not believe that ghosts necessarily want to or even can inflict harm, at least not too much."

"What if you're wrong?"

"Haven't been yet," Chase grinned, turning to see Agent Sohn come in behind him.

"How do you even begin to get into that line of work?" The agent asked as Abigail left to hunt down the mayor.

Chase looked at the agent carefully and replied, "It started with trying to help people. I was teaching a class on paranormal psychology. One of my students was an older student. She had a daughter that was terrified to be in her own room. When she asked me some questions about ghosts and demons, I could see the genuine concern in her face. She was afraid for her daughter. I realized then that there are people who needed help."

"Was the girl's room haunted?"

The professor's face drew pensive, shrugging, he replied, "I don't know. The husband wouldn't allow for a full investigation. He just thought his daughter was angling for attention. I was able to talk to the mother and daughter about taking ownership of the house, not to be afraid."

"How would someone do that?" Danica asked, casting a confused eye at the professor, "Take ownership?"

"Proclaim the house theirs. State that the previous tenants were no longer welcome, perhaps even inform them that they had passed in the first place."

Agent Sohn looked horrified, "So you think that they don't realize they are dead?"

Again, Chase shrugged, "It's a theory. There have been numerous cases where such a proclamation had stopped the activity. Not every case invlolves trying to get rid of the spirit, though."

The FBI agent looked confused, "What do you mean?"

"Some clients like the activity, they just call us in to document that something really is going on and to make sure it isn't something nasty."

"People *want* to live with the ghosts?" Sohn was incredulous.

"They figure they were there first, as long as they aren't hurting anything, they had no problem sharing," the professor replied.

"This ghost thing just gets weirder the more I learn about it. Why would anyone want a ghost in their house?"

Chase took a deep breath, "Not every story is bad, or scary. Some are sad or almost sweet. We were asked to investigate a site in New England. It was an old milling town that had a terrible flood nearly a hundred years ago. When we were doing a question and response with the KII, we seemed to be having a conversation. According to the responses, it was a child, a little boy. He was looking for his family. They were separated when the river crested. He had spent nearly a hundred years searching for his family. His mind hadn't aged. He seemed lonely, sad. We had pretty good evidence that he was following us around the entire investigation. We felt a little sorry for him when it came time to leave."

"That is unbelievable."

"I know. We went back again. He met us at the entrance. We found his family's cemetery plot and told him how to get there. We walked there with a teddy bear and placed it next to his parent's markers."

"And then what? Did he...did he go...wherever reconciled spirits go?" Sohn gasped.

Chase shrugged, "Don't know. I hope so. Reports of activity at the mill stopped."

Agent Sohn shook her head, "You have such a strange job."

Chase smiled. Danica lost herself for a moment in the professor's eyes. There was a charm to him that belied the science-geek persona. Before she could mull the intricacies of Ryder Chase any further, the voice of Mayor Stenner blasted into the room.

"Quite the excitement. Good to see the volunteers at the Fire Department can respond swiftly. Nice to keep their skills sharp," Mayor Stenner declared.

Chase shuffled, "A fascinating addition to an already intriguing case."

"Hmph," the mayor's jovial face cast the slightest scowl. "We any closer to getting to the bottom of it?"

"We're making progress," Chase admitted weakly. "We would like to have the engineers gather another water sample. We have a more complex chem panel we would like to run."

"I thought we already handled that."

Nodding, the professor added, "We did. The widespread mutuality of the symptoms, the groupthink, the psychoneurological reactions all cast direction at some sort of intoxicant. We can re-run air, soil, and crop tests as well."

Mayor Stenner hesitated, "Alright, let's just keep this quiet until results come in. We don't need to rile the town up any further. How is the paranormal angle coming?"

"Obviously something is going on. It is even affecting highly trained investigators. We have nothing definitive, that is why we must continue to explore all possibilities," Chase conferred.

"Well, the weekend is nearly upon us. If we get the sample this afternoon, it's unlikely you'll hear back from the lab until sometime on Monday. If you can spare some time away from Helberg, you might as well join us for Corn Fest. I promise you, it is likely something you don't get in the city," Mayor Stenner offered.

"It may be good for the team to take a step back. Get away from it a bit might allow some fresh theories to make their way to the surface," Chase agreed.

"Well, consider us your hosts," Stenner declared.

Thanking the mayor, the investigators walked out into the bright sunlight. "What do you say, Agent Sohn, a little R & R?"

Danica grinned, "Might take a little convincing for Jeffers, but worth a shot. You might be right. A little separation might help the team form some new ideas."

Jeffers' protests quickly subsided into a relenting sigh, "Fine. The team gets the weekend to regroup. I'm personally hanging my hat on the water thing anyway."

"Corn Fest, huh?" Wally mused, "What is that anyway?"

"You know, fried corn fritters, corn dogs, corn shucking contests...that sort of thing," Tannen declared.

Clapping his hands together, Agent Dunlap smacked his lips, "I aced my last PT, I'm in!"

Jeffers rolled his eyes, "Lock the house down, Professor, can you use that fancy camera equipment for passive surveillance?"

"I can," Chase nodded.

Wally piped in, "We can do better than passive. If anyone enters the house or breaks the digital barrier we set up, I'll get a notice on my phone."

"Alright," Jeffers conceded, "I guess we get a weekend with the hayseeds."

FIFTEEN

To Ryder Chase's eye, the charming farm town only became a more endearing shade of Americana with the start of the festival. Hard-working farmers and laborers found ways to sneak away from their duties, at least for the day. The usually sleepy town was alive with energy. Immaculately cleaned, decorated in a fashion that reflected the patriotic and agricultural spirit of the town, was surprisingly elegant. Chase felt Main Street was an idyllic postcard and snapped a shot on his cellphone.

Concentrating on the screen, he nearly bumped into a figure that had approached on the sidewalk.

"It's impressive, isn't it?" Agent Danica Sohn asked.

Chase stammered for a moment, "Sorry for nearly running you over. Yes, it is impressive. This town has an appeal to it."

"It really does. I never figured myself for a country girl, but the way this community pulls together…it's inspiring," Agent Sohn admitted. After a thoughtful breath, she turned towards the professor. "I sincerely want to help them. Can we…help them?"

Chase sighed, "I think we can."

"Those tests we ordered. You think the answer is in them?"

"I hope so."

"Really? You aren't pulling for some supernatural explanation?" Sohn asked.

"I don't pull one way or another in an investigation. I look for the truth. No different really than the oath that you took when you became an agent, right?" Chase replied.

"True. But I have to say, when we are after a nasty guy, I pull for the case to be against him," Sohn admitted.

Chase smiled, "I guess it would be hard not to."

The professor leaned against a light pole. He watched families hold hands as they crossed the street, lining up for the town parade. "I want to help them too."

"Hey, you two, we have coffee!" Wally's voice sang from across the street. He was followed by Tannen and Agent Dunlap, each with cups in both hands.

"No Starbucks around here, so we swirled in a bunch of sugar and cream to make kind of like a latte," Dunlap added.

"I kind of got used to crappy coffee in the academy," Sohn admitted.

"Ah and Agent Jeffers, even a cup for you," Tannen said, handing the agent, the only one of the group not in street clothes for the day, a coffee. Jeffers slid his sunglasses on as he approached the group.

"I trust you all are enjoying your day off?" the lead agent lobbed his rhetorical reply as he accepted the cup. "What did you do to this coffee?"

"Oh, that was Wally's idea. Adding a little whip cream to it – part of the latte effect," Dunlap replied.

"Hmm," Jeffers grimaced as he took another drink.

Tannen frowned at the lead agent, "Corn Fest have a formal wear portion of the beauty contest?"

"I gave my team the day off. I did not say *I* was going to take the day off. I got up early to catch up on paperwork, that is to say, updated the checklist of reports for Dunlap and Sohn to prepare for our return. Which with any luck ,will be the day those reports come back from the lab samples," Jeffers answered happily.

"You always put a suit on to do your paperwork?" Tannen pressed.

"As I move about town, it is important that the image of an agent remains professional and impartial. You have to maintain an air of respect in the course of an investigation," Jeffers said, taking another drink of his coffee.

The group suddenly started snickering at the agent. "What?" he demanded. Checking his shirt and tie for spillage, he didn't realize that the whip cream in the coffee had left a froth mustache above his lip.

"I can see that, Special Agent Jeffers," Wally said stiffly.

Even Agent Sohn couldn't resist a giggle.

Eying his reflection in Agent Dunlap's sunglasses, Jeffers quickly swiped as his lip, liberating white foam as he did. "Try and hold yourselves with decorum today," Jeffers snapped and turned in disgust.

Suddenly a voice boomed from behind them. "It's gonna be a great day for a festival!" Mayor Stenner strolled up to the group. "I see some of you appear ready for some fun."

"Mr. Mayor, Hope is beautiful!" Danica Sohn said.

"It really is, very admirable sight," Chase agreed.

"We are proud of our little hovel," the mayor beamed, grabbing at his jacket lapels as he rocked on his heels. "Say, Dr. Chase, the parade's about to start, you and your crew want to join me in my car? Love to have you as my guests."

"Very gracious, sir. I think I prefer to take it all in as a bystander," Chase admitted.

"Very well. Anyone else?" the Mayor panned around the group.

"I'll go!" Wally stepped forward.

Agent Dunlap snapped his fingers, "Mr. Mayor, how about your own secret service escort? It'll be a riot! Give me three minutes. I'll be right back...unless...Jeffers, you're already dressed for the part."

"Oh no," Jeffers waved his hands in front of him. "You two idiots can do whatever it is you feel you need to." Under his glasses, the lead agent rolled his eyes and stormed off.

"Tannen? Agent Sohn?" Wally prodded.

"I want to try taking pictures of the parade with my new camera," Tannen shrugged.

Agent Sohn smiled politely, "I think I'm with Ryder. I love watching the town enjoy their day."

"Alright, it's just us two idiots!" Agent Dunlap clapped his hands together and ran for the hotel. "I'll be right there, don't start without me!"

With the investigation team split into their Saturday activities, Ryder Chase found a seat outside of the local tavern and pulled up his notes on the investigation. Having been easily the most intriguing case of his experience, he tried to make sense of it all.

The extent of those affected, even on the investigation team, was unprecedented, never mind the mortal impact. He had never worked a case where death was directly associated. The question that still rang in his mind is what supernatural connection, if any, was a factor. The evidence that his team had compiled was fascinating, but none of it definitive.

The lore of the farmhouse throughout the community was irrefutable. The reality of it on the other…even he had a hard time sorting it out. Possible images caught on the FLIR, spikes in the electromagnetic field detectors, the shared experience with the fire – all absolutely amazing. Yet, he could not declare any of them solid evidence in either direction. Other than the scarecrow, they hadn't found any evidence that would even suggest human involvement.

The scarecrow. What in the heck was that about anyway? Did Wally actually see it? Was it a prank? The evidence they found in the field contradicted itself. Mysterious floating being that hardly left a trace or careful human going to great lengths to do what? How would messing with the investigators benefit anyone? The one who might have had something to gain was the only one with something to lose by attracting suspicion. Chase slid the tablet across the table. The whole thing didn't make any sense.

As he pondered his review, a shadow crossed his peripheral vision. He turned his head to see Agent Sohn standing beside him.

"That good, huh," the agent smiled.

"Oh, just trying to tie everything together, but it is like having pieces from unrelated puzzles and trying to make the picture on the box out of them," Chase admitted.

Sohn shrugged, "Maybe a moot point come Monday. What wasn't in the water might be in the air or the soil."

"Maybe," Chase replied thoughtfully.

After pausing for several moments, the agent asked, "Can I join you?"

"What...oh, sure. You don't need an invitation, Agent Sohn."

"Danica. I'll make a treaty with you. You call me Danica and I will call you Ryder. Fair?" the agent asked. Receiving a nod, she added, "Besides, adding "Professor" all the time has to be as annoying as you adding "Agent" every time you speak to me."

"Fair enough," Chase grinned.

They both looked out at the street and the crowd of families waiting for the parade that was announced by the siren chirps in the distant starting point. Catching the server approaching, Sohn looked at her watch, "Almost noon, I'm buying."

Ordering a hard lemonade for herself, she smiled when Ryder ordered a beer.

"Nice to see these embattled families enjoying themselves," Chase said as he tilted his beer her direction in gratitude.

"It is. I can only imagine how frightening and frustrating this must be for all of them. Death in a city of a couple million is one thing. Several in such a small, tight-knit community...devastating," Sohn nodded.

"Not knowing why it is happening, who might be next. Afraid for their families and neighbors," Chase added.

"Hopefully, today is a lasting reprieve for them," Sohn said as they leaned back in their chairs and watched the oncoming parade.

The Sheriff lead the way, the lights on his cruiser flashing, occasionally letting the sirens sing for a moment announcing their arrival. Chase and his companion took in the scene. Anxious children craned their necks past their parents to see what was coming. Any restraint was lost when the Sheriff tossed handfuls of Tootsie Rolls out towards the curb. Squealing children darted to collect the candy. Chase was most impressed when he witnessed several examples of older children handing over part of their treasure to nearby younger ones.

As the parade rolled by, marching bands from nearby schools trooped past along with clown in little go-carts and horse's ridden by women in ornate costumes. A handful of floats pulled by tractors celebrated winning football teams, businesses, and of course, the Corn Princess and her court.

When the final entry in the parade meandered by, Chase and Sohn could only gawk, setting their drinks down for fear of spilling. Mayor Stenner sat on the seatback of the convertible, with Wally by his side waving the FLIR camera and EMF detector at the crowd. Walking diligently alongside the convertible was Agent Dunlap, fully clad in a dark suit with dark tie. His right hand pressed a corded earpiece into place while scanning the route through dark sunglasses.

Nearly spitting a mouthful of beer, Chase choked, "Oh my...wow."

Agent Sohn, too appeared to fight for words, "Hmm. Those are *our* partners out there."

To their amazement, the crowd cheered wildly as the car passed, much to Wally's enjoyment.

Watching for a moment in silence, their heads followed the spectacle as it traveled in front of them. Chase finally broke the silence, "I gotta say, I am with Jeffers on this one."

Sohn laughed out loud, "At least this case brought those two together. Two peas in a pod."

Almost out of his control, the words slipped out of Chase's mouth, "At least the case brought together…" Stopping short, he prayed his cheeks did not redden, and his intentions blatant as he looked at the agent across from him. Snapping back into frame, he shook his head, "Those two."

Finishing her lemonade, Agent Sohn placed the bottle on the table and fished out a handful of bills. "Shall we? I think I am going to use the town's good humor today to see what else I can find out."

Chase nodded, "I'm not sure these notes will produce anything new, but I'm going to take a final pass through them."

"Then I'll see you around," the agent smiled as she got up from the table.

"Thank you for the beer…and the company." Chase shifted just slightly as he watched Danica Sohn melt away into the crowd, which was filling the park where the festival's main activities were taking place. When she disappeared, he pulled his tablet close and returned to his notes.

The aromas of elephant ears, corn fritters, grilled sausages mixed with freshly strewn straw struck Danica Sohn as strangely pleasant. Perhaps it was olfactory spurned reflections from childhood, or it was just the jubilant atmosphere that permeated the space and the people who milled about it.

Slowly, she strolled through the booths. Games were set up for the children, locals had their stations to sell vegetables, homemade jams and pies or crafts. A stage near the center of town welcomed a quartet to take their places with acoustic guitars while a young woman held the microphone.

Danica noticed the farmer with the land that ran past Helberg was there with his jars of honey and teas. In a little mason jar, next to his drinks, she saw a little bundle of brilliant red flowers that she had never seen before. Curious, on several levels, she strode to his booth.

"Ah, agent. Enjoying our little festival?" the farmer asked.

"Actually, yes. Quite a bit," Sohn nodded.

"That one of your partners I saw escorting Stenner in the parade?"

"Uhh…yes," the agent admitted solemnly.

"Hmm," the farmer uttered in response.

Pointing to the Mason jar, she asked, "I've never seen those flowers, what are they?"

"They're not flowers, they're Thimbleberries!" the farmer replied proudly, "They don't naturally grow out here, so I have had to play and experiment quite a bit to get them to take hold and fruit. Try one." The farmer plucked one of the round berries and handed it to the agent.

"Wow, that is good!" Sohn admitted.

"I have tried many variations to get some of my more unique plants to work. Graft one to another, add certain species of plants and flowers for cross-pollination, determine male versus female plant..."

The agent looked surprised, "I had no idea farming could be so complicated."

"Didn't used to be. Plant a crop, let it thrive, plant another. These days with the government involved and big corporations demanding all of the genetic material get their stamp of approval, takes the joy out of it. That is why I started my little stand. I get to create some things naturally, the old-fashioned way – mixed with a little bit of genuine farming science," the farmer replied.

"Well, your thimbleberry was delicious!"

"I tried to grow enough to make some pies or its own tea, maybe next year. For now, it goes in the brambleberry," the farmer sighed. "Would you like a tea? On the house."

"I appreciate that, maybe later. Good luck today," Agent Sohn said and moved along the aisle of booths. She mulled over the strange little man. He seemed to care about his work genuinely and could be quite pleasant – some of the time. She pondered if he could be involved in the incidents at Helberg. Suddenly, a thought popped into her head.

Rushing back to the farmer's stand, she asked, "Say, I was curious, to get your special plants to thrive, do you use any special chemicals to help them along?"

"Chemicals?" the farmer scoffed, "That's half my battle around here. I don't want any of the junk on my plants or in my soil. You don't need that stuff to make your land work and plants to thrive. Just a little know-how and hard work. I don't use pesticides, genetically modified anything…I guess what you folks in the city would call "organic". I just call it good."

"Then how do you get your special stuff to survive?"

"Knowing what they need. Some fungi carry nutrients from plant to plant. Flowers attract the right kind of bees. Perfect compost mixtures that provide the correct pH and nitrogen levels to the soil. That's my point," the farmer said, jabbing his finger to his skull. "Gotta use what farmers have always known. Cheat Mother Nature, and she'll eventually call you on it."

"I have to say, I admire your passion," Sohn conferred.

"Helberg used to farm that way, before he changed. Then it was all big machines, herbicide, pesticide, trucked in fertilizer. Trucked in fertilizer…can you believe that? We have farms all around. All the fertilizer we could want, never mind the churn from last year's crop, why in the world truck in some tanker truck full of poo processed in some factory somewhere? It took me years to get that plot back in order."

"Do the other farmers around here agree with your way of farming?"

The farmer shrugged, "Some do, some don't. Most don't take issue with it; they just do theirs their own way."

"This has been very educational, thank you."

"Anytime, agent," the farmer grinned. "The offer for tea is open. Just don't tell the men you work with. They have been my best customers."

Danica smiled, "Your secret is safe with me."

For just a moment, Ryder Chase froze in he tracks and did a double-take. As he was strolling through the midway, the professor was surprised at what he saw, and then quickly realized he shouldn't be surprised at all. On the stage adjacent to the musical performers, where the judging was held, Wally sat in the third seat. Fork in hand, ready for the next tasting.

"Corn muffin and corn chowder cook-off," a voice next to him said.

Turning, Chase saw Tannen grinning from behind the protracted lens of his camera. "I see you are documenting this?"

"Oh yeah. You should see some of the shots from the parade; they're hysterical," Tannen laughed. "Ooh, got it!"

Chase followed the direction of the lens to see Wally with chowder streaming from his chin to his shirt. "At least we are well represented," Chase sighed.

"Hey, you are the one who titled him 'Second Investigator'", the EMT chided.

"Assume Medic is a higher rank," Chase assured his friend.

"That come with a salary increase?"

"Double what I am currently paying you," Chase offered.

"You don't pay me," Tannen frowned.

"I know," Chase smiled.

Leaving his medic to capture their teammate in action, Chase set off to wander the festival. He admired the little town. Everyone, including the vendors, seemed happy and relaxed. Other than the wares that stocked in the booths, all of the events and games for the children were free.

"Professor!" a voice called from one of the booths.

Turning, Chase saw a smiling Abigail waving him over. He paused for just a moment. The inquisitive receptionist looked different. Her hair was draped over her shoulders, allowing her loose curls to bounce in the breeze. She wore a long, flowing white sundress that cascaded down to her sandaled feet. Resting her glasses on her freckled nose, she was in her element. Radiant.

"Hello, Abigail," Chase offered.

"I'm so glad you guys got to come to our festival. What do you think?"

Chase took the scene in for a moment. "You know, I am impressed. This is the positive vision of small American towns that we all think of at the core of our country."

Abigail frowned for a moment. "Do you always talk like that?"

Chase blushed for a moment, "Sorry, years speaking to Academia kind of taints people after a while. I love how the town comes together. The kids get to play for free; the community brings the best of what they do and who they are to the forefront. It's like a big, happy family reunion."

"Just missing the family scandal and the drunk uncle, but it's still early," Abigail grinned.

"So, what are you showing off today?" Chase realized the unfortunate timing of his question as his eyes rested on the pendant dangling in the bosom of Abigail's scoop neck of her dress.

"You like it?" Abigail asked.

Chase felt his cheeks redden at the question, his eyes darting around for something else to fixate on, finally coming to rest at the freckles magnified through her glasses and then to her brown eyes peering through them.

"I made it myself. That's what I do in my free time. I make jewelry out of almost any kind of stone or metal," Abigail said, gingerly rubbing the pendant she wore around her neck.

"Uh, yes. It is striking, really eye-catching," Chase scrambled.

"I don't suppose you wear much jewelry," Abigail eyed him, "How about a lady friend back home?"

"No, not really," Chase admitted, feeling little beads of sweat well up on his forehead. He hadn't, until now, seen the Town Hall receptionist as anything other than a busy body. But here, she was sweet, confident, and alarmingly attractive. The way she peered at him, there was little room for doubt that she was attracted to him. Yet, something was nagging at him to refrain.

"They are lovely," Chase said, looking across Abigail's display. "Your craftsmanship is exquisite."

"Thank you," Abigail beamed. "You don't have to buy anything. I just wanted to show you."

"Thank you. I'm glad you did."

"I assume you'll be around tonight? I'll save you a dance!" Abigail smiled big, her eye sparkling behind her glasses.

"Uhm, yes. Maybe I'll see you tonight," the professor acknowledged and shuffled away. He wondered if his cheeks felt as red as they felt. He marched forward through the midway, half curious to turn around, but refusing to. Chase maintained a steadfast exit away from the park and out of the festival grounds.

SIXTEEN

Special Agent-in-Charge Jeffers avoided most of Hope's festivities. In truth, it had less to do with his lack of appreciation for the town's charms, but rather he refused to allow his focus to be swayed. Early in his career, he was working on a similarly innocuous case. The objective was to stake out a gangster in Miami Beach. The three-month-long assignment often had periods of downtime.

One weekend when the subject was known to have been out of town, he and his fellow agents let their guards down. Most of them young, they enjoyed the chance to blow off some steam. Most of their time spent in a little room listening to every word muttered in the gangster's house, nearly all of it non-pertinent, the beach and bars of Miami were attractive outlets.

Midway through the evening, the subject came back. His trip had not gone his way, and he was in an enraged stupor. He smacked around his girlfriend and called in his man who had set up the deal. The deal that was supposed to come back to Miami for the FBI agents to intercept. The man had been pulled in by the investigation team and given asylum for helping them bust his boss.

Slamming his girlfriend to the floor, the gangster tipped over a table its contents spilling to the floor. His cellphone case opened up, revealing a tiny wire attached to the battery. Picking it up, the man studied the device. Ripping the wire free, he threw the phone across the room.

Freeing his gun, the boss swung it wildly around the room. Eyes wide, he focused on his number two man. Pulling the trigger, he began gunning down everyone in the room. By the time the Jeffers' team could come together and react, everyone in the house was dead, eight people in all. They caught the man as he was gunning his Ferrari down the driveway.

The agent-in-charge that day was demoted and reprimanded. As a subordinate, Jeffers' record was unscathed, but it was a lesson he would never forget. He loved his job. It was duty with sacrifices. Sacrifices he knew about before he signed up. When he was on a case, it was business – until the report hit his director's desk.

He didn't mind the team spending their day with the people of Hope. He could almost feel a little envy towards them. But Jeffers remained vigilant, focused on the case. He had Wally set up his computer and cellphone with the electronic barrier alarm and even a video feed of Helberg House. From his room, he could review case notes and monitor the house.

Reviewing each death, noting the coroner's remarks. Noting any connections to the victims, especially that crazy farmer. He marked their proximity and known activity near Helberg just for the sake of notation. As he connected the dots, he was alarmed at what his last task identified.

Every victim had been in the vicinity of Helberg, at the very least passing by, prior to their deaths. Leaning back in his chair, he rubbed his temples. "There had better be something in those tests!" he muttered to himself.

Wally and Tannen made their way through the bustling carnival. Don Tannen was busily chewing a corndog down to the nub of the wooden stick. "Sure, you don't want one? Nothing like homemade corndog...well, I assume the dog isn't homemade," the EMT asked between bites.

Wally patted his stomach, "I don't think I'll eat for a week."

Tannen grinned at his friend, "You looked like you were going to puke by the time you got to the last judging round."

"I don't know how those guys do it. And that little old lady judge…I saw her eating an elephant ear after that. What the heck?"

"Uhh, they work harder than you?" Tannen chided.

The tech scowled for a moment and then nodded his head, "Yeah, they probably do. Tough buggers out here in farm country."

"Yes, we are," the barker for the ring toss game agreed. "Care to give it a try? Game's on the house."

Wally started for a second and then stopped, "Hey, aren't all the games free today?"

The barker laughed, "Can't pull anything on you, boys, eh?"

"I'll try!" Tannen chirped in.

"Alrighty. The objective is to hit the…" the barker began as he handed the paranormal investigator three rings. Before he could finish, Tannen let all three rings fly. One after another, they all spiraled down the neck of the gold bottle.

"Well, I'll be. We have a winner!" the barker said. Reaching for the most gigantic stuffed toy, a four-foot-tall giraffe. Tannen didn't hesitate and gave it to the nearest child walking by.

Wally looked at his partner, stunned. "Give me a shot at that!"

"I don't have any grand prizes. Didn't expect to give one of them away today. At least not until the raffle at the end of the fair," the barker admitted.

Wally concentrated. Holding the first ring, just pass his nose, he focused on the gold bottle. Letting the ring fly, it sailed through the air. Clipping a clear bottle, about a foot from its intended target, it bounced and careened entirely off the table and onto the ground.

Frowning, the tech readied for his next shot. This one tossed Frisbee style. The ring skimmed off one bottle and then another, like a skipping stone across a lake, and also landed on the ground.

"What the...," Wally stomped and scowled. "The trajectory of the arch, given the weight of the ring, the diameter of the opening..."

The barker and Tannen burst into laughter. "We're laughing with you, not at you," the barker promised.

"But I'm not laughing!" Wally moped. Tossing the ring over his shoulder, it hit the lip of a red bottle, bounced over a blue bottle, and then finally wedged itself between a pair of clear jars.

"You think too much, young man," the barker suggested.

"Tight rotation, no arch, and oh yeah…" Tannen grinned, "Skill."

Wally shook his head in disgust. His sour mood heightened when a young boy walked up and landed his first shot on a blue bottle.

As the barker handed the boy the remainder of the rings, he asked, "You fellas find what's been causing all the trouble around here?"

"It has been a tough case," Wally admitted. "I'm sorry for the town's losses."

"We lost a lot of good people," the barker said he reached for a medium-sized prize.

Tannen felt for the man. He didn't notice that all festival-goers within earshot had stopped what they were doing and cast their attention at the conversation. "There are certainly some things we have struggled to explain. We think we have a theory," the EMT admitted.

"Oh? We've been looking for answers for a while," the Barker pressed.

"We have some more tests coming in. We hope they will hold the clues to what has been happening to people…your town," Tannen shared.

"Tests?" a man next them asked. He pulled his son, who was admiring his stuffed prize close. "You mean the samples Stenner had the crew gather yesterday? We've done tests. You've done tests. That place is evil. Whatever happened to the Helbergs, they were once good people…whatever happened out there…that's the reason. You people were supposed to come in and take care of it."

"It's not as simple as that," Wally defended, "There may be something out there, but there may be other explanations too. We have to explore…"

"Charlatans!" the man spat and walked off with his son.

Wally, Tannen, and the barker looked at each other, stunned for a moment.

"Ah, don't listen to him. We know you have a job to do and such," the barker offered.

"I don't blame him," Tannen admitted. "Your town has suffered such loss. Any delay, any lack of swift, decisive solution must be frustrating."

"At first, everyone looked for a real-world answer. When none came, all that was left was the spiritual. I suppose they expected some magical exorcism or something," the barker said.

Wally looked at the man, "We'll do what we can. I promise."

"I know you will, son," the barker smiled. "Good luck to you, boys."

As night descended on the small town of Hope, the lights took over the park. The carnival rides and their neon danced in wild, strobing rhythm. The booths were cast in soft glow from strung bulbs, which gathered at a peak in the center of the park. The stage had its own lights, showing off the band and spilling onto a fast populating dance area.

In a dark corner of the park, a little gazebo built in commemoration of the town's bicentennial served as a quiet overlook for Ryder Chase. Leaning his back against one of the posts, he drank in the scene. As happy as the town seemed during the day, it appeared even more jubilant at night.

Young girls smiled at boys who shrunk from the dance floor. Husbands and fathers swung wives and daughters alongside the band. Friends gathered at tables and sang along and laughed. Chase smiled as he watched a young man escort an elderly woman so she could have a view of the dancers.

Abigail swirled by herself, as radiant at night as she had been in the day. Chase had to admit she had a spirit to her. Yet, his resolve to remain in the shadows was solidly resolute. Watching the town in their celebration, he almost jumped when footsteps sounded behind him.

"A beautiful evening," a smiling Danica Sohn stated as she walked towards the professor.

"It is. This town, so easy to discount it when you first come upon it. The people here... they are *really* good people," Chase said, studying the crowd.

"They are," Agent Sohn agreed. Pointing to the rail Chase was sitting on, she asked, "May I join you?"

"Please," Chase nodded.

"I think Miss Abigail is waiting for her dance partner," the agent watched as the town hall receptionist swayed to the song.

Chase grinned, "You spying on me, *Agent* Sohn?"

"I might have overheard her in the park today. She has been gushing over you since we arrived here," the agent defended.

"I'm sure there's a dance partner for her out there somewhere," Chase suggested. "He just doesn't happen to be right here."

"You don't dance?"

Chase looked squarely at the agent. Almost in spite of himself, he replied, "With the right partner..."

For a long moment, the two stared at each other. Chase lost his breath for a second, watching the carnival lights sparkle in the agent's blue eyes. He overthought each move she made at that time. The slight rise in her eyebrows, the wetting of her lips with her tongue, the most minor shift forward. Closer.

Drawn, almost as if by some invisible force, he leaned forward. What little breath remained in him was gone as she too closed the gap between them. With a nervous swallow, he allowed the magnetism to reel him towards her. He could feel the warmth of her breath as her lips began to part, coming ever so close to his own. Suddenly overwhelmed by her - so attractive, confident, yet endearing...

As they closed together, the anticipation of embrace, simple admiration stoked to a searing, curious passion. Their cellphones simultaneously burst into life. Instinctively, they pulled back, hesitated for a moment, and relented to check their 9-1-1 text alert.

Agent Jeffers sipped a cup of coffee while he peered over the top of this laptop screen at the sports highlights. He was quite removed from the sports scene, but enjoyed the few moments of downtime he mustered to check in on his favorite team. Grimacing as the Red Sox outfielder slid under the tag of the Yankee catcher, Jeffers flipped the television off. As he did, he noticed a change to the laptop screen.

The perimeter warning along the front gate of the Helberg House began to flash. The audible tone started beeping its alarm. Switching his view to the security camera, a shadow began to stretch into view, and then another and another. Soon, half a dozen townspeople passed the security camera placed just off of the front porch. The first man turned to address the group, holding a gasoline can in his hand.

In an instant, Jeffers pulled up the text display on his phone and alerted the team.

Within a minute of the text, the investigation team had gathered by their vehicles. "There is a mob gathered at the Helberg House. We've got to go, now!" Jeffers said, climbing into the SUV. Agents Sohn and Dunlap barely inside the vehicle, the lead agent had the truck in gear and was speeding down the road. In the SUV's mirrors, the paranormal team's van kept pace.

The vehicles' engines roared as Jeffers led the response. Their rental cars lacking sirens, the agent flashed his headlights as he flew past the one vehicle they encountered on the road. Whisking by the roadside stand, he kept the pedal slammed to the floor until they were just alongside the Helberg House.

Several people in the crowd had lit torches while the man in the security video was opening the can of gas. Jumping from the vehicle, Jeffers had his firearm in his hand and a tactical light shining at the man's face. "Hold it right there!" he shouted as the investigation team joined him.

Chase ran up to the porch with his hands out, "Wait, wait!"

He positioned himself between the gas can and the house, "I get how you feel. I'd feel the same way if my neighbors, my friends, my family were stricken the ways yours has. I'd be angry and confused and impatient."

"What do you know about any of this? Any of us?" the man holding the can snarled.

A voice from the crowd joined him, "Yeah, you waltz in here, the big expert. You don't know anything!"

"Except to have half of your team running out screaming for one thing or another. What was it, a scarecrow?"

"Imaginary fire?" another piped in.

The man holding the gas squared up in front of Chase.

"You don't want to do this," the Professor warned.

"Oh, I'm pretty sure I do. I heard them talking at the fair. You don't know what's going on. More tests. Tests that have already been done. This place is evil, and we're going to burn it to hell!" the man swung the gas can along the wall of the porch to cries of excitement from the crowd.

"Yes! Yes, burn it to the ground," Chase encouraged and then waved his hands, "When the investigation is over.

Maybe that is just what the town needs. And you know what? That might even be the answer."

Chase turned to face the crowd, "But if the answer is somewhere in this house. The answer to why the people in this town are getting sick, why you are losing them, why you may lose more, then we *must* find it. I don't want your town to lose anyone else. We will get to the bottom of this. Maybe it is in a test. Maybe it is some heartbroken, angry spirit somehow locked in this place. Whatever it is, we *will* find it!"

Chase paused to study the reactions of the crowd. The agitated, desperate faces he saw when he first launched himself on the porch softened. The man with the gas can looked undecided. Jeffers remained unflinching; his gun aimed directly at the man who shared the porch with the professor.

"When we do and when we know your town is safe. Burn it down. Put this sad place to rest. Give my team a little more time. You'll have your answers. You'll have your peace," Chase assured.

The man next to him screwed the cap on the gas can and set it down. To Chase's surprise, the man burst into tears. Turning from the crowd, he wiped his eyes. "I lost my wife. My son lost his mother…" he choked.

"I'm sorry," Chase said softly.

"Find out what happened to her. Find out how to keep my son safe, because, I...I don't know," the man dropped the can and silently walked down the steps, through the crowd that had fallen mute, taking in the exchange. As others watched, he made his somber march to his car, turned the key, and turned the wheel towards town.

One by one, the townspeople followed suit. A few thanked the investigators, most remained silent. Their loss hung heavy in the air as the investigators watched the last car drive away.

"Quite the speech, professor," Jeffers recognized.

Taking in a deep breath, Chase sighed, "We have to help this town."

SEVENTEEN

Breakfast the next day saw a different team of investigators. They were bright, positive, and cohesive. Even Jeffers was in a strangely jovial mood. When pressed, he grinned, "I have my bags packed, I'm ready to wrap this one up and get the heck on a plane out of this place!"

Chase leaned into the breakfast table, "A little confident about the results…"

"It's the last only thing that makes sense," Jeffers reasoned, "Unless you're going to tell me otherwise."

"No, it has the highest probability. We have mixed evidence to suggest the paranormal. Nefarious human intervention hasn't shown itself to be a viable angle, save for the rogue scarecrow," Chase admitted.

"The scarecrow thing still bugs me," Jeffers agreed. Suddenly he snapped his fingers, "Unless there is a connection – whatever the toxicology report says, maybe someone wanted it covered up."

"Or just someone pranking us," Dunlap suggested.

Agent Sohn shrugged, "The investigation has attracted a lot of local attention. It may have just been someone wanting to get the scoop. The scarecrow thing may have just been a convenient way to sneak behind Helberg."

"Might not have been a scarecrow at all," Chase offered. "With all of the nuttiness we experienced out there, false fire alarms, shadows attacking agents…it could have just been a person, and whatever is affecting people got to Wally that day."

"I have been strangely susceptible on this case," the investigator admitted solemnly.

Pushing his plate away, Jeffers suggested, "I think I am done. You'll call when Tannen is back with the report?

"Of course," Chase nodded.

The lead agent waved for the check. The waitress advanced to the table, "This one is on the town, guys. We all appreciate your help."

"That's real good of you," Wally exclaimed. "By the way, I thought you had the best corn fritters."

The waitress beamed, "Aw, I'm glad you liked them. If I am going to come in second place, it outta be to Sally

Winters. She's the one who gave me the recipe years ago. Who knew then she held back on an ingredient or two."

"A little cayenne pepper, I think. Very subtle, but nice kick," Wally suggested.

Snapping her fingers, the waitress exclaimed, "That must be it. I'll have to try that!"

As the waitress walked off, Ryder Chase reflected on the mood of the town and of the team. The scene this morning was in stark difference to when they first arrived. Jeffers was even pleasant, smiling as he left the café. As Chase thought about the report, he hoped all that goodwill wouldn't change.

"Well, maybe Agent Jeffers is right," Wally said, getting up from the table, "Time to pack all that gear up and be ready to go."

Dunlap nodded and followed the paranormal investigator out of the diner.

Dr. Chase and Agent Sohn accepted refills on their coffees.

"You were quite impressive last night...," Sohn suddenly shifted in her seat and spat, "With the crowd... at the house, I mean."

Chase paused for a moment observing the agent in a rare moment of awkwardness and then shrugged, "I felt for these people. Imagine if our families and friends were dropping for no apparent reason."

"It must be absolutely awful for them," Sohn admitted.

Chase nodded, "Could hardly imagine. I might want to burn the place down too."

"You hit it on the head, though," Sohn said thoughtfully, "It would be empty without answers, and if destroying Helberg took away knowing what happened...or if it could happen again, that would be much worse."

Danica Sohn sat back, taking in the magnitude of their conversation. Watching the professor equally pensive, "About the gazebo, I...we..."

Before she could finish her sentence, Don Tannen burst in the door. Waving the packet of documents in the air, he called, "Gather the crew. We've got to go over this!"

The investigators gathered in the board room of the town hall. The mood quickly thickened as the visage of Don Tannen did not convey positive results.

Jeffers was nearly climbing out of his folding chair, "Well?"

Pulling the stack of papers out of the clasped envelope, the medic dropped on the table in front of him. "The results are pretty clear. The fertilizers used are all USDA approved, air quality out here is as expected exceptional, the water – which we have already tested – is clean. Not even naturally occurring anomalies are present. At least not on even a micro level that could impact the people here," he informed the group.

"Nothing? Not even a trace?" Jeffers demanded.

Tannen shook his head, "Not really. Traces of stuff – naturally occurring phosphates, mineral particles, calcium – but all things you would find on any farm, garden, or municipal water supply."

Jeffers slammed his fist on the table, "Damn! Back to square one. I am so sick of this place!"

The investigators all looked at one another. No one quite sure how to respond.

"I'm about ready to chalk it up to demonic possession just to put a stamp on this thing!" Jeffers cursed.

Wally's eyebrows lifted, "Really?"

The cross look Jeffers returned in reply left no room for misinterpretation.

After a long delay, Tannen spoke, "Maybe it truly is haunted. It is just too hard to capture definitive evidence. That is why, after thousands upon thousands of hunts, investigations, reported evidence, there is such debate. We are dealing with the intangible. Trying to humanize evidence in an inhuman circumstance."

Other than a huff from Jeffers, the room was silent.

"I don't know," Chase admitted. "I think we have to continue doing what we started when we came here. My team investigates the paranormal, continuing to pry at plausible reasons for the tragedy here, and the Agent Jeffers, you and your team keep running through untoward human interaction."

"Fine," Jeffers said definitively. "I guess this meeting is done. You head to the house with your team. I think my team will flip over the most obvious stone – farmer Stilton."

When the group disbanded, they nearly collided with Abigail. The city receptionist had planted herself as close to the door as possible. Jumping back as she heard the chairs sliding out, she could resist hanging for every last tidbit.

"Oh, hi," she smiled, looking at no one other than straight into Chase's eyes as she spoke. "You are interested in Stilton? I may have some information for you." Guiding Ryder Chase away from the group with her hand just under his shoulder, she took a few steps down the hall.

In a soft voice, she whispered as she stared at Chase, "I heard from Iona Coffey that Brazelton, he's the man who led the mob, had been suggesting burning Helberg House down, but he couldn't do it himself. When he overheard how angry Brazelton was, the poor dear, Stilton pressed him on the idea. It didn't take much to encourage his action." As the receptionist whispered, she moved as close to the professor's ear as she could. Her breath was tickling him.

The investigation crew watched, shocked at the blatant singling out of the paranormal researcher. Agent Sohn scowled as she looked on.

Chase looked uncomfortable at the violation of personal space. He shrugged slightly at the group. Sohn was unsure if it was meant directly for her or the entire team.

"Well, that is useful information, thank you, Abigail," Chase stated as purposely flat as he could.

The receptionist beamed at his praise.

"Uhm, well, we had better follow up on that," Chase said, pulling away from her.

"Let me know if it turns up anything," Abigail called as Chase made a hasty exit, his team in tow.

"Actually, useful information," Jeffers said as they exited the town hall.

"Hmmph," Danica Sohn rolled her eyes. "We already know about Stilton. She was stating the obvious from cramming her nose to the door listening to us."

"Yes," Jeffers nodded. "But her witness testimony gives us probable cause."

Pulling up at the roadside stand, the FBI team marched up to the snoozing farmer with determination. "Jamie Stilton," Jeffers called to the man whose face remained hidden beneath the wide brim of his hat that was pulled down. "We have a warrant to search your premises."

Without lifting his hat, a voice replied, "You didn't need to get a warrant, all's you had to do was ask. But if you don't mind, what exactly is it you are looking for, and maybe I can help you find it."

The farmer's reply struck the investigators odd. While the casual presence could have been delivered to throw them off track, the man sounded genuine.

"Actually, things will run a lot more smoothly if you stay out of our way," Jeffers stated. "If we have any questions or need access to something, Agent Dunlap will let you know." Ordering the junior agent to remain near the farmer, Jeffers and Sohn headed for the barn.

Down an arching path from the house, the barn was separated from the house by a little triangular patch of grass that had been largely taken over by clover and dandelion. "Maybe herbicide is not the issue. He clearly has not used any here," Jeffers quipped. My hunch is if he is adding something to the soil, he is storing it in an outbuilding somewhere."

"Make sense. The water table charts show the aquifer the town uses for most of its water supply runs has tributary somewhere between this farm and Helberg," Danica Sohn answered.

"And then we have our culprit!" Jeffers added.

Agent Sohn paused as they reached the enormous door of the barn. "But if that's the case, why hasn't he had any issues?"

"I guess it would either mean he is doing it on purpose to get back at the town or to stake some land grab at Helberg, or maybe he has some immunity to it," Jeffers shrugged.

"Like how some people suffer from allergies where others don't," Sohn nodded. "We'll have to have the pathology lab run a scan on potential allergens and cross-match them with the symptoms of the victims."

Flipping on his flashlight, Jeffers peered into the musty barn, "We should have thought of that sooner."

The barn was a cluttered space. A large tractor sat directly in front of the door. Beyond the farm machinery was an array of tools, buckets, stacks of wood, and rejected house clutter. "Not exactly a neat freak," Sohn observed.

"We'll have to pick through it all," Jeffers was defiant, playing his flashlight diligently throughout the entire barn. When he saw a door at the far end, he picked up the pace.

Flipping a latch on the door, he swung it open. A loud groan echoed as the room was revealed. Burlap and polypropylene bags lined tow walls. Canisters and glass jars filled a row of shelves against the far wall. The remaining wall housed a worktable. Half-empty canisters and containers littered the top of the bench and all the space surrounding it.

Pulling a penknife from his pocket, Special Agent in Charge Jeffers began gingerly poking through the contents. "Wonder if the labels are what they say…Spinosad…diatomaceous earth, pyrethrum…I think I know what that one is. Steinernema carpocapsae…what the…" Jeffers sighed as agent Sohn poked her head in the door. Looking up at her, he looked frustrated, "I don't know what any of this stuff is. We need to pull in some help!"

EIGHTEEN

Wally wheeled the van in front of the Helberg House. Ryder Chase studying the house as always did upon arrival, swore he saw something flash by the upstairs window. The image was fleeting. The change of light as the van turned into the drive could have easily accounted for an illusion. Deciding to say nothing to his team, he made a mental note to check it out after they unloaded what gear they chose not to leave behind.

Chase and Wally carried cases of their instruments into the house while Tannen stayed in the van to boot up the monitors and the computers. Unlocking the front door, Wally pushed his way into the Helberg house. Setting the case down, he snapped open the latches and selected the gear he wanted to use.

"You aren't going to like this," Wally warned as he dug into the bottom of the case and withdrew a small plastic box.

"What?" Chase asked absently as he grabbed a voice recorder, a video camera, and an EMF detector.

"I'm using the 'kit'," Wally replied.

Patting his pocket to ensure his flashlight was in tow and turning off his cellphone, the professor responded, "What kit…oh! The kit! You know how I feel about the kit."

"It is a bonafide tool for paranormal investigations," Wally defended.

"But…you don't know what doors you could open. We aren't qualified for that, and if this does turn out to be that, I will withdraw us from the case," Chase declared.

"Come on, Ryder. Several clues point that direction. If there is a door here, it is already open," Wally was steadfast in his resolve.

"But demons, I don't even want to think about it. I'm not sure they even exist…"

Wally grinned, "Then you will have nothing to worry about."

Shaking his head, Chase grabbed his gear and headed upstairs. He couldn't be sure, but he thought he heard soft footsteps and scurrying as he ascended the stairs. As creaky as they were, the force they applied through the infrastructure of the old building was enough to scatter weird creepy noises though out Helberg. Moving on, he made a beeline for the room he thought he saw a figure move by when they arrived.

Video camera rolling and EMF detector held out front, Chase carefully stepped down the hall and into the room. First, panning the camera around the space, he was satisfied it was empty. Next, he ran the EMF detector around the entire perimeter. Barely showing anything on the display, Chase was satisfied the room was clean.

Suddenly a faint scraping sound caught his attention into the closet. Running the EMF sweep around its opening, he turned the handle and peered inside. His flashlight aided the camera sweep. The closet was clean. Even the EMF detector refused to register even a blip on the screen.

As he walked away from the wardrobe, a cracking noise ran the length of the ceiling, seemingly snaking its way through the entire third floor. Staring up, Chase wondered what his partner had awakened.

Wally went to the lowest part of the house. Finding a clear spot in the basement, he opened the plastic box and began setting up an array of items. Before getting started, he turned on the night vision camera to record his work. First, he pulled a small pouch of red brick powder and made a circle around himself. Within the ring, he drew a second circle with white chalk and then began drawing a star inside it. Lighting several candles surrounding the first circle, he began speaking to no one in particular at first, then started calling out names from a list.

He wasn't sure, but it seemed when he reached Maggie, the flames on the candles dimmed, if just for a moment. "Maggie?" he called again, but this time received no specific response. Finally, calling Maggie again, it was if the house erupted. The ceiling shook. Slightly at first and then pounding. Dust showered, and cobwebs danced as Wally shined his flashlight up in the air.

With a wide sweep, Wally scanned the entire basement for signs of a presence, shadow, or anything else that might catch his eye. As the pounding drew nearer, he swore he heard horrified, pained scream in the distance, almost as if it were traveling through the home.

"Maggie? Is that you? I am not afraid. I do not like what you are doing to the visitors of this house, the people of this town. I command you to leave and never show yourself here again!"

At that moment, the pounding increased and culminated with the front door of the house, slamming shut so hard that the building shook. For a moment, there was silence. Then the sound of normal footsteps coming from the floor above.

Soon the door to the basement opened, and the disturbed face of Ryder Chase stood in his flashlight beam. Wally grinned at the professor, "Did I banish the demon?"

Clad all in black, the young man checked his watch. He hoped they had at least a couple of hours. Waving his group forward, he crept to the edge of the cornfield. Peering at the back of the Helberg House, he scanned the windows with his binoculars.

"Mason," he whispered, "Check the driveway for cars!"

Nodding, the young man named Mason, moved further along the field until he could see the driveway. With a thumbs up raised in the air, he grinned at the leader.

"Alright," the leader in black called softly, "When I watched them last, they set cameras around the perimeter. One captures the back yard, one the front porch, and the other the driveway. The cameras only reach so far, but if we stay to the northeast corner, we should be clear of the video and passersby on the street."

"Jace, how are we going to get in?" a girl, dressed similarly in black.

"Good question Caroline, I jammed the bathroom window on the second floor shut with a couple of washers. From the inside, it would just seem like the window was frozen shut. Ready?"

With nods from Mason and Caroline, Jace led the trio out of the cornfield to the corner of Helberg House. Stacking a pair of pallets that had been half rotting in the weeds, Jace carefully climbed up to the window. With a screwdriver, he wriggled the sash of the bathroom window until the washers shot free, showering down to his friends below. "Sorry!" he hissed.

Using the screwdriver to leverage the window, slid it opened and crawled inside. Turning, he hung halfway out to give his friends a hand. Once they were all inside, he asked, "Isn't this place cool?"

"This is going to be awesome!" Caroline nodded.

Mason also nodded as he silently took in the old place. From his backpack, he pulled out a flashlight and a handi-cam. Pointing the camera at Jace, he pointed his finger and flipped the "record" button.

Jace beamed and straightened himself. "Bismark Paranormal is looking into the mysterious Helberg House. This has been a site of terrible tragedy out of which was born a horrifying blight on the quiet town of Hope, North Dakota. The result of sadness and pain that occurred on this property appears to be laying siege on the people of this town, who are reputed to be dropping dead in fright."

Disappearing from the camera, he took a quick swallow of his drink. Popping back in the frame, he continued, this time with a KII in hand, "We are here to find the truth behind these occurrences, a mystery that has even federal investigators baffled."

To his team, Jace called, "Come on, guys. My reports have activity happening all over this house. We'll start up top and work our way down."

Leading his team down the hallway, he turned upstairs and landed on the third floor. The KII really the only tool in their arsenal other than the video camera and slim digital camera held by Caroline. Jace held the instrument in revere. As he walked, he shared a long diatribe about EMF and the ability of the KII to find and even communicate with spirits.

Watching Jace scan the ceilings, Caroline asked, "What are you looking for?"

Turning first to Caroline and then to the camera, Jace responded, "Attic access. Starting at the very top. Not ferreting out the nooks and crannies of a haunted location is a frequent error of investigators. Poking into a front bedroom, Jace scanned the ceiling. Finally, in the closet, he let out a triumphant fist pump.

Looking around for a moment, Jace turned to Mason. "Lace your fingers together and give me a lift!"

Slipping hit foot in the clasped hand of his friend, Jace launched himself to the ceiling of the closet. Pulling a small notch in the wood, he lowered the cover on its hinge. Sweeping his flashlight around the attic, he nodded confidently, "Looks clear."

Hopping back to the floor, he continued the investigation. Moving from room to room, they canvassed the third floor. Just as Jace was going to urge his team down a story, Caroline called out to her friends. "Uhh, van in the driveway!"

Jace darted to the window and watched the researchers grab cases from their black van. Cursing to himself, Jace whispered instructions to move quickly to the stairwell. As they reached the top step, the front door swung open, and they could hear voices from below.

"We'll have to wait them out!" Jace hissed. Tiptoeing, the crew moved carefully to the room with the closet they had found the attic access.

To their horror, footsteps began making their way up to the second floor, turning on the landing and heading up to the third floor. Pointing up, Jace urged his friends into the attic. First boosting Caroline up and then Mason. After closing the closet door, Jace used Mason's stretched out arms to pull himself up. Sliding the hatch back into place, the crew huddled.

The heat in the attic was oppressive. Sweat ran down each of their faces, and their bodies seemed to radiate heat. Each of them sucked down their drinks despite their best effort to ration them. Pressing her ear to the hatch, Caroline listened to the shuffling on the floor below them.

Jace and Mason also strained their ears to hear anything that would encourage them to believe the researchers were leaving or about to locate them. Mason touched Jace's arm and shined his flashlight across the expanse of the attic. Jace looked up with a questioning frown.

"Thought I heard something," Mason whispered. Playing his flashlight back and forth, he was finally satisfied nothing was there.

A moment later, Jace snapped his light on in the same area Mason was searching. "I think I heard it too!"

"Yeah, but this time closer!" Mason nodded.

Keeping a light on, they stared in the empty space of the attic. Jace tugged at his collar. The stale air was stifling. His skin began to itch, and his tongue was dry. Emptying the last of his drink. He waited.

"There's nothing there," Jace finally muttered and turned off his light. Checking the illuminate hands of his watch, he realized it had only been minutes despite it feeling like an eternity.

Suddenly the noise was closer. As he and Mason reacted, Caroline perked her head up. Both Jace and Mason turned their flashlights on. "It was right here!" Mason rasped, circling his flashlight only a few feet away.

The hair on Caroline's neck stood on end as she watched her teammates react. A noise behind her caused the lights to whirl in her direction. Refusing to look herself, the girl felt her skin sear and then drop ice cold.

Jace launched himself onto the hatch, his weight dropping him into the closet. Holding his arms up, he accepted Caroline. Mason followed, and the three raced out of the closet, down the hall, and leaped several steps at a time down the stairs. Colliding with one of the researchers, Jace felt powerful hands grasping his shirt. The trio tried desperately to squeeze by and complete their escape.

"Hold on there, guys!" the voice of the researcher commanded.

"We have to get out of here!" Caroline pleaded, tears streaking down her face.

Mason squeezed through and bolted out of the house.

"We are in danger!" Jace squealed and tried to wrestle away.

"I believe you. My team and I can help you," the researcher said. "Come with me. Your life may depend on it."

"You are Ryder Chase," Jace stammered as he was marched down the steps.

"I am."

The rest of the walk was in silence. Dr. Chase marched the pair out to find Don Tannen corralling Mason. "You three might be in real danger. If your friend there will stop struggling, my associate and team medic Don Tannen may be able to help you," Chase declared.

"It's alright, Mason, he's right," Jace called.

Mason stopped flailing and allowed Tannen to help him up.

"He's burning up!" Tannen said as he escorted his captive to the van.

"These two feel hot too," Chase replied. "Of course, they have all been hiding in an attic."

"We're sorry. We just wanted to investigate…" Caroline stammered.

"The face…the face…" Jace shook himself.

"Face? What face?" Chase asked.

"We heard noises. Each time, they were closer and closer. Next thing you know, a face appeared behind

Caroline. We freaked and uh…ran into you," Jace explained.

"Did you see the face too?" Chase asked Mason.

"I saw something. An old man, I think."

Jace looked incredulous. "It was a girl. The Helberg girl!"

Tannen and Chase shot each other glances.

The medic continued his triage of the would-be investigators. "Their heart rates are all up. They are dehydrated and likely have heat stroke. I am going to have EMS pick them up. They need fluids and have a full cardio panel done up on them."

Nodding, Chase added, "I'm going to call it into Jeffers as well. They should know."

"They can get the results of the med panels too," Tannen agreed.

With Tannen providing cold towels around their necks and bottles of water to the young trespassers, Chase went to locate Wally and fill him in on the day's events.

"So…I didn't conjure a demon?" Wally asked when the investigation team had convened that evening.

"No, thankfully not. A few kids who won't be poking into an ongoing investigation anytime soon," Chase replied.

"Were you able to get the results of their labs?" Chase asked.

Agent Jeffers nodded, "In return for not pressing charges – breaking and entering, interfering with an ongoing investigation…among others – they gladly agreed to waive any HIPPA patient confidentiality rights." The agent tossed a packet in front of the professor, who handed them to Tannen to review.

"What did you guys turn up today?" Chase asked.

"He had a bunch of chems locked in his barn, but it turns out they are all typical of a certified organic farm. We tore the place apart, but found nothing. He is still top of my list. He must have a stash somewhere else," Jeffers replied.

"We had every chemical and combination of chemicals Stilton uses on his farm. Nothing really all that dangerous, at least not in quantities that would work their way into food, water table or aerated from his farm," Agent Sohn added.

"That's too bad…" Tannen declared from behind the hospital reports. Seeing the team cast frowns at him, he corrected himself. "I mean, it would help explain this. It appears that these kids ingested some kind of chemical. The elevated temperature, increased heart rate, delusions…it screams of a drug."

"Delusion," Chase repeated. "Did you notice how the two boys had different visual experiences? The one was adamant he saw Maggie Helberg. The other was pretty sure he saw an old man."

"Multiple ghosts? Demon who morphs?" Agent Dunlap suggested.

Chase chuckled at the idea coming from someone other than his team. "Sure, I suppose, but I really don't think so. I'm not saying something isn't going on there, but at the least, I am suggesting that what is reported being seen or heard is not necessarily what was there."

"Like a hallucination," Jeffers suggested.

"Or whatever is driving this preys on what is in the beholder's predisposition. In the case of the kid who researched Helberg a bit, he expected the girl and low and behold; the girl was there. The other kid probably assumed what anyone else might who didn't know the intimate history of the place – an old farmer, why not see his face in your vision," Chase elucidated.

"Maybe both were there?" Wally asked.

Chase shook his head, "No. I pressed them on that. They each saw only a singular image; they just obviously didn't match."

"Multiple spirits," Wally shrugged.

"I don't know. Something just doesn't seem right. Too much hasn't been real," Chase protested.

"Like burning buildings that weren't really on fire."

"Exactly."

"Did the kids say they took anything?" Tannen asked.

Jeffers shook his head, "It looks like we need to pay a visit to our young friends."

"Mind if we tag along?" Chase asked.

"I suppose you could prove helpful, deciphering the rants of your own kind." The FBI team leader led the way to their vehicles.

By the time the investigation team arrived at the hospital, the three young researchers had appeared to return to normal. They drug around handheld vital signs monitors with them, but were free to move about the hospital. Securing an empty boardroom, Jeffers' team ushered them in.

"Your labs have returned with basic chemical compounds for drugs similar to ecstasy," Jeffers stated as the wide-eyed kids stared at the FBI agent. "You guys been popping happy pills?"

Jace screwed his face into a not, "No! Not at all."

His compatriots echoed his reply.

Jace sipped his ice water nervously.

Jeffers put his foot on the arm of a chair and leaned into the trio, "Then how do you explain your labs?"

"I...I don't know. I swear..."

"Uhm, do we need a lawyer or something?" Mason asked.

Jeffers sneered, "Depends on if you have something to hide."

"Look, we shouldn't have gone in there, alright, man. Especially knowing you guys had been brought in on the case. I just couldn't resist," Jace said.

Caroline, "Yeah, I mean, if we were able to solve a case that perplexing for Dr. Chase, whoah!"

"Yeah," Mason nodded. "We were nervous the first night. I thought we were caught for sure."

Jeffers head snapped, "First night?"

"Yeah. We were checking out your scene...from the cornfield," Jace added.

"Cornfield..." Dunlap rubbed his chin. Before he could spit it out, Wally jumped in.

"That was you in the cornfield!" Wally steamed.

"Yes...yes, sir," Jace stammered. "We wore those little booties like repairmen wear in your home, so we didn't leave any prints. We tried using the stalks to make sure we didn't. Mason looking like a scarecrow, was merely an accident. Caroline and I were able to duck out of sight. He wasn't so lucky. We overheard the fuss about a scarecrow, and we nearly laughed ourselves into being caught!"

"Great!" Wally scoffed in disgust.

Jeffers couldn't resist laughing at that one. "That was you! I knew the scarecrow thing was idiotic. I was sure it was that crazy farmer."

"So, no partying in the last few days? No hallucinogens, smack, a little date, or party night 'X'?" Agent Dunlap confirmed.

"No. I mean, we've snuck the occasional beer, but no drugs…ever! Besides, when we are on a case, we take ourselves very seriously," Jace defended.

"Well, you got something in your system somehow," Dunlap declared.

"If we did, it wasn't anything we did on purpose," Jace swore. "Is it possible there is some kind of mold or something in the air in that house? We felt fine until we were in there for a while."

"We checked the air," Jeffers nodded. Turning to Tannen, he asked, "We check for mold?"

"No, but not a half-bad idea. Mold spores are known to do all sorts of crazy things to people. They frankly don't match the chemical properties found in these guys, but who knows," Tannen admitted.

"Worth a shot. When we get back to town, we'll scrape some samples," Chase agreed.

"Not bad, kid. You learn to get permission for your locations before you hunt, you might just make an okay investigator," Wally crooned.

NINETEEN

As the group walked back to their cars, the FBI team's cellphones went ballistic. Each grabbing theirs, they read the incoming message. Agents Sohn and Dunlap looked at Jeffers, receiving his nod, their expressions grew serious, and their pace purposeful.

Jeffers filled in the paranormal group, "Amber alert out of Fargo. A tan sedan heading north on Highway 29. We'll meet up with you later. If you see a car matching that, give us a call immediately. We are going the same way we came, find a different route to see if they change direction."

In a flash, the FBI crew was in their black SUV and wheeling out of the parking lot. Tannen had already pulled up his maps program on his phone and instructed Chase, who jumped in the driver's seat. "Out of Fargo, take route 200. It is not as direct as the highway, but it will parallel

Jeffers' route. If the kidnapper zigs our way, we might see them."

Special Agent-in-Charge Jeffers placed the small red LED flasher he used when traveling on the dash of the SUV. Gunning the engine, he quickly found the highway ramp and sped west. In the distance, a huge thunder cloud loomed, slowly making its way east.

"They have a chopper in the air? Out here, it should be pretty easy to pick a vehicle," Jeffers said.

Dunlap mashed a couple of buttons on his found and called the regional office. After a brief conversation, he shook his head. "They fired a bird up, but the air is too unstable. A massive weather system is heading our way."

"It looks pretty dark up ahead," Jeffers acknowledged, peering at the sky above their windshield.

Agent Sohn read off the report, "Eight-year-old girl from a little town not far from Finley. Her family was shopping in Fargo. They turned for an instant, and she was gone. Store cameras caught a man rushing the girl out of the store. She wasn't going willingly, and customers in the parking lot tried to subdue the man, but I guess he got violent and thrashed them pretty good."

Sohn's phone beeped in another message. She read, "Suspect is medium skinned, 5 foot eight, thin mustache male. Possibly a nomadic worker connected to a rash of sex crimes in three other states along the pipeline."

As Jeffers led the big SUV down the left lane of the freeway, he gritted, "Let's make this his last!"

The rain began to fall. Just a mosaic of waterdrops dancing across the windshield, then with increased intensity and size of the drops, the storm started to show its rage. "This is not going to be helpful!" Chase mused from behind the steering wheel.

"It's like the start of something terrible about to go down in a horror movie," Wally chirped, "And that is coming from a ghost hunter."

"What kind of creep would mess with a kid," Tannen asked.

"The worst kind," Chase instantly spat. His focus was intense on the road ahead as the tires fought for traction on the rain-soaked streets, and gusts of wind hammered at the side of the van.

Tannen's phone suddenly started buzzing and beeping wildly, much like the FBI agents with the amber alert. "Tornado warning," he shared. "Looks like the evening is going to get a little bit worse."

"Keep your eyes peeled for the suspect vehicle," Chase commanded. "It is all I can do to see the road and keep us pointed in the right direction."

Wally nodded from the front seat, and Tannen stuck his face close to the window in the passenger row.

Driving as fast as he felt safe, the professor guided the van for the intersection with the road Jeffers was heading down.

"Air support has been called off until the storm passes," Agent Sohn said as she scrolled through the messages on her phone.

"He'll be long gone by then," Jeffers grumbled, pushing the SUV even harder.

Carving his way through the traffic, which had slowed with the reduced visibility. Finding the exit for the rural highway and tracked north. The raindrops mixed with hail thundered against sheet metal of the SUV, lightning split the sky followed by an enormous boom.

"Poor girl," the lead agent muttered as his eyes fought to follow the blacktop. Sohn shot a surprised glance at her partner. She had not often heard empathy from the all-business special agent.

"Call from Sheriff Biggs in Hope. They have a roadblock north of Chase's team," Dunlap reported.

"Good. That narrows the playing field," Jeffers replied.

The quiet highway was silent with other motorists. The storm had gotten so bad, the few cars on the road had elected to pull over and wait it out. With great skill and the help of a useful traction system, Jeffers kept his speed up while his team scanned the cars on the side of the road.

As the SUV whooshed down the highway, it screamed towards an intersection. A pair of headlights sliced through the torrent as it too closed in on the crossing. "That's Chase," Agent Sohn confirmed texting Don Tannen, "They have not seen the suspect car."

"Tell them to station themselves there. Put on their hazards and block the whole damned road," Jeffers commanded as the SUV rocketed past. With a straight, clear shot, Jeffers squeezed his foot on the accelerator. Despite his years of intense training and experience, he could help to get a hint of an adrenaline lift.

Eating up highway voraciously, it did not take long for the team to see flashing lights up ahead.

Snapping at her phone in disappointment, Sohn shared, "That's Sheriff Ira Biggs. No one has come through."

Clicking off the traction control, Jeffers stabbed at the brakes while snapping the wheel around. The big SUV skid sideways. Moving from brake to accelerator, Jeffers powered the SUV while returning the traction control. Scrambling for grip, the truck caught the edge of the highway before the tires found the pavement, allowing Jeffers to straighten out and barrel back the way they had come.

At the intersection, they found Chase's team as ordered - spanning the east pathway. "Tell them to stay put!" Wheeling the SUV, Jeffers took the road west. The wind had grown so loud; they could barely hear. "Storm is right on us!" Dunlap bellowed.

Ignoring the report and the weather, the lead agent refused to let up on the gas.

Pointing, Agent Sohn asked, "What's that up ahead?" A swath of corn adjacent to the highway had been mowed down.

Easing off the pedal, Jeffers brought the SUV in for a look. From the edge of the road, the earth had been torn up. A rough path had been chewed into the cornstalks. Wincing from the wind and rain, Sohn shone her light through the open window. As the beam cut through the wall of raindrops, it revealed a car resting on its roof, steam spewing from the engine bay.

Jeffers swung the SUV so that the lights were directly on the vehicle and jumped out, his firearm at the ready. Instantly joined by his junior investigators, they flanked the car. Sohn and Dunlap took opposing cover positions while Jeffers kneeled to the ground, searching the car.

"Empty!" Jeffers shouted through the rain.

Standing by the field of corn, Agent Dunlap called, "Tracks! They went this way!"

Joining him, Sohn and Jeffers followed a pair of muddy footprints into the field. Lightning menaced all around them, and they had to lean against the wind to make headway. Danica lost her footing, sinking her arm elbow deep into the mud. Frustrated, she hauled herself up and inspected her weapon.

"You alright?" Jeffers shone his flashlight in her direction.

Offering a quick nod, she urged them to move on.

Nearly a mile off the road, they came to a path splitting the field in two. Scanning the ground, it was unclear was a new track or an indentation from the rain. "Dunlap, head east, Sohn, try and see if you find a trail here, I'll go west."

The worst part of Jeffers' decision was that it took him directly facing the slant of the rain. It hammered at him mercilessly as he made his way down the tractor rut. Moving his flashlight along the ground, he thought that he had found a pair of matching tracks to the ones they had followed from the road. In case he was wrong, he did not call on his team to follow.

The path was arrow straight, allowing Jeffers to cheat in following the tracks. Through a moment of sky engulfing lightning, he saw the silhouette of a building up ahead. Stepping off of the trail and into the sea of corn, Jeffers used a more cautionary pace as he approached what looked like an old barn. As he reached a small clearing, another flash of lightning confirmed a large, old barn. Dark spots dotted the building, indicating to Jeffers windows or missing boards that would provide anyone inside with a view outside.

Circling the barn, Jeffers found a section that appeared relatively intact. Timing a sprint in between flashes of lightning, Jeffers left the cover of the cornstalks and flattened himself against the wall of the barn. Barely audible above the noise of the storm, Jeffers heard sobbing. He couldn't be sure, but given the circumstances, he had to hedge his bets that the girl was in there.

Inching along the wall of the barn, the agent found one of the openings. As lightning blazed across the sky, he could see a little girl huddled against a pole in the barn. A few feet away, her captor was capturing the moment on his cellphone camera. Watching the man take pleasure in the little girl's fear made Jeffers' blood boil.

With each subsequent flash that lit up the sky and the barn, Jeffers took precise steps forward. In the light, he observed the man and the girl. In the respite between lightning, the agent strode steadily forward. His gun drawn, Jeffers appeared in the doorway. As a streak of light silhouetted him, he saw the man jump towards the girl. In another flash, Jeffers saw a glint of metal in the man's hand.

In the return to darkness, Jeffers sprang quickly. When lightning struck again, he could see the man with his bladed hand pressed against the crying girl's throat. The man gawked at the doorway, trying to locate the man who had been standing there. Once more bathed in darkness, the standoff grew tense.

In a mighty flash of multiple streaks of lightning, the man once more scanned the barn. Just as the light was about to return dim, to his horror, the man found the shadow from the doorway. The snout of a .45 caliber was staring back at him. His knife hand twitched. The corresponding crack was not of thunder, but the agent across the room neatly delivering a fatal shot into his forehead.

Snapping his flashlight on, Jeffers sprinted across the barn. Ripping the man's arms off the girl and tossing him aside, the agent scooped up the girl and pulled her away from the scene. Leaving her alone for only a moment,

Jeffers returned to the rogue worker. A check for weapons and a pulse, satisfied the agent walked calmly to the hysterical girl. Holding her close, he called it in.

When Agents Sohn and Dunlap arrived at the barn, they were initially taken aback by the scene. To see Jeffers wrapped up, gingerly caring for the girl. Exhausted from the ordeal, she had nearly fallen asleep against the agent's chest. To see the oft steely partner of theirs in this position, furthered by his breach of protocol not having called them in sooner, was remarkable. Jeffers was the staunchest, by-the-book agent they knew.

In a soft voice, Jeffers cooed, "Agent Sohn...would you take Addie?"

Stirring at the arrival of the two other agents, the little girl complied.   Jeffers was unsure if she felt safe with them there, or she was just all out of fight. "Poor, little thing," the agent muttered as he watched his second in command lead the girl out of the barn and away from the scene. The rain was still falling heavily, but the van with the paranormal team jounced its way along the tractor trail to the barn.

Opening the doors to the back, Sohn and Addie ducked in. Tannen was already with his medical gear.

"Hi there..." Tannen began as he started to look the girl over.

"Addie," Sohn reassured.

"Addie, I know you have been through a lot, I just want to make sure you are not hurt. Are you sore anywhere?" the EMT probed while checkIng the frightened girl's vital signs.

Addie shook her head "no". Her humongous green eyes so exhausted, even the fear and sadness had given away to plain old fatigue.

"A little dehydrated, let's get a drip in her before the locals arrive so she can get some sleep," Tannen suggested as he saw the line of flashing lights in the distance.

"So... what happened?" Agent Dunlap asked, analyzing the scene.

"Found the barn. I didn't want to call you guys in and off of your searches until I could confirm. By the time I did, I had to act. The suspect moved to the victim with the knife. I had position and dropped him."

Dr. Chase and Wally stuck their heads in the barn. "Is he...?" Wally began.

"Dead?" Dunlap finished as he duplicated the check on the suspect's vitals.   "Oh yeah."

"The girl is safe. Nice job, Agent Jeffers," Chase extended.

"Yeah, well, it would probably have been better to have allowed him to face a judge and Addie's parents," the agent replied. "Certainly not sorry for an animal like that, however."

"True as that may be, let's not share that little pearl with Internal Affairs," Dunlap suggested.

Outside, a small contingent of police and rescue vehicles pulled up next to the barn. As Sheriff Ira Biggs entered the barn and the ambulance crew conferred with Tannen, loud sirens filled the night.

"What is that?" Wally asked.

"That is our night about to get even worse," the Sheriff elucidated, "Tornado sighted and close. Everyone huddle inside the barn down at the base of a wall! The biggest concern is flying shrapnel. This old barn isn't the best choice, but it is the best we've got."

Chase and Jeffers helped Tannen and Sohn get Addie settled in. Wrapped in a blanket, the crew filled in around her. If the barn collapsed, they would take the brunt. Outside, the wind howled. Rain, corn, dirt, and anything else the storm could find was hurled at the decayed walls of the barn. The roof shuttered, and loose boards rattled, a few flung from their rests and strewn to the other side of the barn.

The wind crescendoed, growing from a roar to a shrill whistle. Rain found its way through the holes and cracks. Lightning strobed in the sky. The crew remained vigilant in their pose, even as a portion of the wall next to them gave way, boards pelting their backs and their hands protecting their heads.

As quickly as the chaos whirled around them, the whistle slowed. The roar moved away from the barn and those inside. Soon, all they were left with was rain and the occasional thunderclap. Eventually, they too began to dissipate.

"Everyone alright?" Sheriff Biggs called out.

The sound of boards tossing aside followed with a chorus of "fines".

"Addie, hon, I think it is time to get you home," Danica Sohn cooed to the girl.

"You see her all the way there," ordered Jeffers. He had hoped to go along himself, but as the shooter, he would have to stay for the investigation.

Sohn nodded, "I will."

"Oh no," Sheriff Biggs gasped as he listened to his radio. "Page, a little town south of here, took a near-direct hit."

"Anything we can do to help?" Chase instantly piped up.

"Take all the hands I can," the Sheriff nodded.

Sohn grabbed the bundled Addie in her arms. "I'm taking the SUV. The regional bureau has a team en route, and the medical examiner will be here soon."

"We'll be fine. Get her home," Jeffers waved his hand at the agent.

Dunlap was carefully removing the damage from the storm to reveal the crime scene as much as possible for the forensics review. Good shoot or not, the FBI would want thorough documentation.

Chase and his crew jumped in their van and followed the police car. Behind them, the paramedic van also trailed.

TWENTY

The scene as the crew arrived in Page was surreal. Aside from an arching transformer and a nearby tree set ablaze, the town was shrouded in darkness. The road into town was blocked by a collage of tree limbs and a pile of what was once someone's fence. Beyond the roadblock, little orbs of bouncing light dotted the town like fireflies. Chase quickly realized the town had taken up arms with flashlights to combat the dark while they searched for their families and neighbors and friends.

Through the police cruiser's spotlight, the extent of the damage could be seen. One side of the street, engulfing nearly a dozen homes, was leveled. Neighbors from the remarkably unscathed opposite side of the road were migrating over to find those that needed help.

Tannen wasted no time grabbing his medical kit and setting up a triage station with the rescue crew. Chase and Wally rummaged in the back of the van, exiting armed with the FLIR and Infrared cameras along with pockets full of flashlights.

Following the Steele County Sheriff, the investigators entered the town and approached the first house closest to them. Wally aimed the FLIR at the pile of rubble, methodically following an imaginary grid, combing the entire building. Chase scanned the IR camera with its night vision at the debris field, searching movement as Sherriff Biggs carefully pulled material off the pile.

"We have something...someone!" Wally called, seeing the telltale glow of 98 plus degrees the FLIR screen. Pointing to a section of the rubble, he directed the Sherriff. "Two, no...three someones!"

Chase set the IR camera down and set up a flashlight with extending tripod legs pointing at the area Wally described. Carefully, the professor helped the Sherriff remove roofing materials and paneling away from the house. Digging through layer after layer, they reached the first inhabitant. Trapped underneath a mattress that covered a table supported by sturdy legs, a shirt sleeve eagerly flagged them down.

Tossing the bedding aside and lifting the end of the table, they revealed three relatively unharmed victims.

Huddled together, they shared the space packed uncomfortably.

"You never think it is going to happen to you. Thank you so much," the woman gasped.

"Are you all okay?" Chase asked.

Simultaneously, the family inspected each other and themselves. Aside from a sundry of scrapes and bruises, they were in remarkably good shape. When Chase offered to have Tannen give them an official once over, they refused, wanting to join the search for their neighbors.

Moving over to the adjacent house, the crew emulated their last search. "I think the Andersons were down with the Donovans," the women they rescued said.

Wally swept with the Flir anyway. Just as they were about to move on, Wally caught a heat signature. "Whoa, whoa. I think one of the Andersons stayed home," he declared. "Right by the back of the house!"

The team scrambled to the rear of the building. Hearing faint whimpering, they pulled material away as fast as they could without causing any of it to dislodge on whoever was trapped. Piece after piece of debris stripped away. Finding a pocket in what was once the kitchen, the crew found the source of the cries. "Ralphie!" the neighbor called.

In the corner, wedged between the refrigerator and the stove, a nervous white and brown spotted terrier huddled away from the rescuers. "Come on, Ralphie, come on!" the neighbor called.

When the dog remained in its spot, Chase cautiously crawled in. Not wanting the floor to cave in or the strange, frightened animal to react defensively, the professor tested each movement. Talking softly to the dog, he used its name, "Come on, Ralphie. I'm not going to hurt you. I'm a friend." Inching forward, he held his closed hand out for the dog to sniff.

"That's a good boy…," Chase urged softly. Reaching out, he gently grabbed the dog and pulled him out from his protective spot. Hearing the dog yelp as Chase's hands held it, the professor realized why the dog was so reluctant to leave its spot, its right hind leg was injured. Avoiding the leg, he carried the dog out to the youngest member of the neighbor family.   "Ralphie has a little injured leg. Think you can bring him over to the ambulance over there? I am sure my friend Mr. Tannen can do something for him."

The child nodded eagerly and carried the dog off for treatment. Chase quickly spun, he realized Wally and Sherriff Biggs had already moved on to the next house. Leading the neighbors over, they found Wally highlighting a spot deep in the debris. "Solid signature right about here," Wally informed the group.

"Hello?" the rescuers called, "Can you hear us?"

With nothing but silence in return, the group shared a heightened sense of urgency. Digging into create a possible path, flinging broken pieces of furniture and siding and roofing materials aside, the crew worked quickly. A deafening, blood-curdling creak shattered the night, freezing the rescuers in their spots. "Stop…stop!" Wally flailed his arms desperately. "The structure that is holding this floor up is failing."

The one group took steps back and out of the rubble. Their flashlights danced along the piles, trying to find a way to continue making progress without endangering the inhabitants. Suddenly Chase had an idea and sprinted for the van. In a few moments, he returned with a reel and a pair of cases. Wally snapped his fingers, "Boroscopes, genius!"

Wally dropped to his knees and opened one of the cases. Quickly he snapped a device to one end of the reel and switched on a monitor. Feeding one end into a gap in the debris, he watched the monitor as the camera of the boroscope snaked its way into the house.

On the other side of the house, Chase probed the much shorter hand boroscope into structural points of the material pile. Looking over Chase's shoulder, the neighbor stopped him, "Go back! Right there. See that? That is the structural beam from the second floor. Keep scanning. It overall looks intact."

Carefully finding entry points in the rubble to inspect the beam, they were able to confirm that the beam was in good shape. Positioned directly above the inhabitants, they hatched a plan. If they could find a way to insert a cross member, they could try and lift the roof and second-floor material off of the strained portion below it.

Completing the inspection, the investigators were surprised when they looked up. Hundreds of people had gathered around the house, trying to find a way to help. "All these people live in this town?" Chase asked.

Scanning the crowd, the Sherriff replied, "Unh uh. Looks like families from Hope and Finley and Colgate…"

"Wow," Chase gazed out, genuinely impressed. "Well, let's put them to work, that's why they came. We need a tractor, maybe two. A backhoe of some sort, some heavy-duty chains, a pipe or pole that can support a few thousand pounds, long enough stretch from here to…say where the front porch started."

In an instant, the crowd had broken up. Tractors rolled in from neighboring houses and farms. The owner of a grain elevator construction company ran with his sons to fetch a truckload of materials. From out of nowhere, a backhoe wheeled down the street. The family of the local grocery store opened their doors and began toting carts of bottled water out for the rescuers and retrieved victims.

From overhead, a helicopter screamed towards the town, its powerful searchlight sweeping through the streets. Setting down in a nearby field, agents Jeffers and Dunlap jogged over to join the effort. Working as a single organism, the pieces of the plan started coming together. Massive metal posts used for erecting catwalks connecting grain elevators positioned as longitudinal support for the building. An armada of farm equipment closed into position.

Carefully, the front and back of the pile inched upwards, just enough clearance allowed a pair of combines to nudge the catwalks under the rubble. When the ends protruded out the back of the house, they were looped with massive chains that hung from bookending backhoes. Diesels screaming, they lifted on the supports. Tense moments crawled past as loose, smaller debris showered down through the two lower floors. To everyone's relief, the cross-beam structure was working!

A quick run with the boroscopes gave the rescuers enough confidence to slip under the elevated mass to try and reach the victims in the basement. Chase, a volunteer firefighter, and two farmers shimmied into the rickety first floor, carefully following the course described by Wally on the big boroscope. Testing their movements, concentrating more on the impact of slipping rubble on the victims below than for fear of falling through themselves. Chase used the FLIR to pinpoint their drop point nearest the victims. Finding the basic structure of basement stairs, they carefully made that their route. The fireman jumped down first, followed by the farmers. Chase lit the way for them with a high lumen tactical light. Following, Chase tested each step carefully. Twisted under the crushing weight when the roof and second floor dropped, it felt as though the entire stairwell could fall.

Swinging the FLIR through the basement, Chase was able to highlight the first victim. The fireman carried a long steel bar. Finding a rafter pinning an unconscious child, he handed the bar to the closest farmer. Using leverage, they were able to free the first victim with relative ease. Leaning down, the fireman assessed the victim. The child was breathing, but it was shallow, his heart rate was low.

"There's no way to get a basket snaked down here. We will have to maneuver the best we can," the fireman said. Using a neck collar, they did their best to minimalize any harm of moving the child. One of the farmers climbed up to the first floor. Passing the child up, the farmer retreated as carefully as he entered, meeting Don Tannen and another EMT where they entered the house.

Chase, using the Flir, located the remaining victims together under a large pile of HVAC pipes and subflooring. Using leverage and teamwork, they began carefully removing debris off of the victims. When they slid away the final piece of ductwork, pipes, and wood, they found a man and a woman huddled together. As the fireman assessed them, he found something else. Between them was an infant. The image before him – a sweet baby, wrapped in a blue blanket, his face covered in dust.

The fireman searched desperately for a breath, the faintest of pulses. A look of horror washed over his face. "I can't find a pulse. He's not breathing!"

Chase slid in next to him, calming the stirring mother and focusing his attention on the infant. Checking the baby's upper airways, he proceeded to provide CPR. As Chase completed the round of compressions and breaths, the fireman rechecked for vital signs. The look on his face told Chase all that he needed to know. Determined, Chase went back to work.

"Joseph?" a weak voice rasped. "Joseph!"

"Jennifer, he'll be okay," the farmer answered.

"Benjamin?"

"We already got him out, he's safe," the farmer assured. Seeing her eyes fall on her husband, his face and arms bloodied, he added, "Ron is okay. A little roughed up, but he'll be fine."

"When the roof fell, he sent Benny towards the stairs. He tried to shield Joseph and me...oh..." she covered her mouth as she watched the two men urge her baby back to life.

In between reps, a sound shattered the night. A sweet, heavenly sound. Baby Joseph gurgled, choked, and then let out a pleading cry. Chase let out a huge sigh and maneuvered out of the way so that mother and baby could be together.

Relieved, Chase and the firemen set to work on Ron. "Pulse is steady, he's lost a bit of blood, and I'll bet one hell of a concussion, but he will be okay. Ron's a tough one," the fireman reported.

Addressing the mother, Chase said, "We have to get you guys out of here." Spying a board roughly the size of the baby, he snatched it. Using a blanket, he saw sticking out of the rubble, he shook off the dust and laid the board on top of it. Putting the baby down, despite angry protests from the very functional set of lungs, he wrapped the second blanket around baby and board, tying it together like a burrito. "Not happy, but we can get little Joseph out of here safely until he can be properly treated."

Nodding, the farmer held the baby up while Chase climbed up to the unstable first floor. Reaching down,

Chase helped Jennifer up. "Be real careful. We have taken the stress off, but this level has sustained a great deal of damage. See that post right there? Carefully scoot over to that, and I will bring Joseph up."

The weary mother crawled over to the post as instructed. The farmer heaved the complaining Joseph up to Chase. "Joseph, hush baby, it's okay," Jennifer cooed.

Chase just casually smiled, "Nonsense. That is a wonderful, beautiful noise. Joseph, you go on and tell us exactly how you feel." Chase carried Joseph with him as he met up with Jennifer. "Okay, we're almost out of here. See that little slit right there? That is your new front door. Follow that path as much as you can, and it will be safe."

Nodding, Jennifer crawled on her hands and knees through the rubble. The dust kicked up all around her, causing her to choke. Hearing Benjamin's voice outside propelled her forward. Feeling fresh air in front of her, she pushed her way through the opening and out to Tannen and the growing team of medics. Waving them off, she pointed to Chase crawling through with Joseph." Please check on Joesph."

"He was non-responsive, no heart rate, no breaths when we found him," Chase reported amidst Joseph's wails.

Tannen smiled assuredly, "He seems to have found his breath. I met Dr. Tierney. He says he is your family doctor. He just gave Benjamin a stamp of good health." The EMT pointed towards an older man at the ring of the crowd.

Behind them, they heard scuffling from the house. A terrible creaking rocked the night, followed by what remained of the house listing. An explosion of wood and metal resounded a cloud of dust, and wood shrapnel shot out from under the elevated portion of the house and ruble. Chase knew exactly what that sound was – the stairs had finally given way. He darted towards the opening, but stopped. To his surprise, he saw Ron on his feet, supported by the fireman and the farmer. Slipping out from under the created entry point, they stood and faced the crowd.

The community of Page rejoiced. Families reconnected. Rescuers received severely needed water and medical attention themselves. Ryder Chase, exhausted-physically, emotionally, intellectually- leaned against the fender of a tractor and watched the town and its neighbors. He was blown away by the response. Friends and neighbors, families rising in the face of tragedy, horrible destruction. Facing fear, pain, and loss together.

When he looked out at the street, hundreds of people supporting each other. Those who could operate machinery did. Those with the strength to lift the enormous burden of the debris did. Those with a medical capacity did what they could. The rest opened their homes to provide a

place for displaced families to stay. Store owners opened
their stores, not to sell but to allow their neighbors in need
to take what they needed. The local diner was cranking out
pot after pot of coffee. Others wheeled out patio grills and
were lining up hot dogs and hamburgers – everything
needed provided by those who could.

Danica Sohn found Chase weary and in awe. "You
okay?"

The professor glanced over at the agent, a
profoundly welcome sight to him. "Amazed really."

"Saving babies?"

Chase wrinkled his face in a way that revealed his
dimples, "Well, that too. This town...and the surrounding
towns. Look at what they accomplished in such little time
together. No FEMA. No Red Cross. Just people who care,
didn't hesitate to do whatever it was they could."

"Kind of gives you hope in our country...humanity,"
Danica agreed.

"That it does," Chase sighed, leaning back on the
tractor.

The pair watched the neighbors take care of each
other and the rescuers who had come in. Exhausted, but
adrenaline and the spirit of the people drove them on. They
had done a lot, but there was still more to do.

TWENTY-ONE

It was daylight by the time every house, every crumpled barn, and toppled tree was inspected. A count of the town matched the response team's tally. Two churches banded together to make a pancake breakfast for the residents and the rescuers.

As Chase's crew with Agent Sohn dove into their plates, Agents Jeffers and Dunlap walked up to the group. "How did you guys fair last night?" the agent in charge asked.

"Exhausted, but it was very rewarding. These are good people," Agent Sohn responded.

"Little Addie reunited with her parents okay?" Jeffers asked.

"Yes. They were, of course, relieved, as was she." Sohn replied.

"I know it's rough, but we will need to spend some time with her collecting the full story," Jeffers said. Responding to the look of concern washing over Sohn's face, he assured, "We have a child psychologist flying in. We will work in the confines she sets up. She won't be grilled, just see if she can't fill in some of the events. Given there's no need for a trial, it can remain fairly high level."

"Good. Poor thing has been through so much."

"Looks like you guys had a rough night," Jeffers studied the group through his own red eyes encircled with dark rings.

"This place got hit pretty hard. Chase and his team were pretty handy. All that crazy equipment was quite helpful in the storm's aftermath," Sohn shared, beaming at the paranormal team.

"Maybe the bunch of nerds aren't so useless after all," Jeffers grinned.

"Aw, Jeffers, tell me that in the morning," Wally quipped.

Agent in Charge laughed, "Yeah, it's probably just the exhaustion speaking."

"On that note, should we head back to town?" Agent Sohn asked.

They all took a moment to assess the scene. Chase agreed, "I think we have done all we can for now. I think being so tired; we may likely do more harm than good at the moment." Turning to his investigators, he patted them on the shoulders, "Nice work, guys."

Danica Sohn looked up at the professor, "We made a pretty good team tonight."

"I think we did," Chase nodded.

It was noon before anyone in either crew stirred. The people in the little town of Hope seemed to go on as if they hadn't been up all night. They had jobs to do and they managed to stifle their weariness to go about them.

For the investigators, their task at hand almost seemed trivial compared to the perils of the little girl and the storm-ravaged town of the previous evening. That feeling vanished when Sheriff Biggs found them at the diner. "I'm sorry to interrupt lunch, but we found another victim. Someone must have used Helberg to ride out the storm."

As the group rose from the table, Jeffers asked, "Do you have ID?"

"We are running that right now. My deputy drove by and saw a car parked outside. He didn't go want to go inside, but he didn't find anyone in the car. He called out, when no one answered, he went inside. Right there on the stairs, he found the victim."

"I see," Jeffers said, trying to make sense of it.

Walking quickly to their vehicles, Tannen asked, "The conditions the same as the others?"

"I don't know yet. I was hoping maybe you could help us with that one," Biggs admitted.

With the Sheriff's car in the lead, the investigation team made their way once more to Helberg. Their vehicles joined the victim's sedan, the deputy's cruiser, and an ambulance. Deputy Rogers was quick to meet the group.

"Sheriff, I called the ambulance, but as I said when I called it in, I'm pretty sure we're too late," the deputy said as he led the team to the Helberg foyer.

Two paramedics were assessing the victim at the foot of the stairs. One of them looked up, excitedly, "We have a pulse. A weak one!"

Tannen studied the victim, a man who appeared to be in his late forties, "What's his heart rate? Temp?"

The EMT frowned at the response as the paramedics loaded the man on the stretcher. "We'll administer epinephrine and monitor him on the way to Fargo General," one of the paramedics replied.

"What is it?" Chase asked.

"If Helberg claimed another one, this is totally different. This man seemed to be hypotensive, not hyper.

More of a case of shock and distress than fear," Tannen answered.

"What does that mean?"

Tannen shrugged, "I don't know. Just saying his condition doesn't fit what we've seen. He needed an epi-boost. Most of the others were flushed – too much adrenaline. He had no symptoms of hyperthermia, almost the opposite."

"Ghost changing its M. O.?" Wally asked incredulously.

By now, the FBI agents were homing in on the conversation. As if reading their minds, Chase responded, "I never said a ghost was killing anyone. The question was, could a spirit somehow indirectly cause a reaction that results in death for those that had an extreme experience."

"So, could people have different reactions to the same stimuli?" Wally surmised.

Tannen nodded, "It is possible."

"It's also possible someone driving through last night's storm that nearly leveled half a town did hide out here, soaking wet to the bone and became ill due to exposure," Jeffers piped in.

"That is a genuine possibility. His symptoms seem to fit that criteria," Tannen agreed.

The Sheriff, who had stepped out while the paramedics loaded the victim and tore off for the hospital, came back in after checking his radio. "The victim seems to be from Minot, couple hours north near the Canadian border. Since his vehicle is facing south towards town, I assume that is the way he was traveling."

"Towards town...," Chase pulled on his lip.

"We'll have to see what the assessment at the hospital has to say. Hopefully the victim will recover and might have some information to help us," Jeffers said.

"Anyone still hungry? I only ate half my sandwich at the diner before the Sheriff got us. I think I'll see if the farm stand is open," Wally declared. The rest of the group paused for a moment, "What? I don't care if he is our lead suspect. He makes great tea!"

Chase snatched his phone and stepped out onto the porch. Fumbling in his pockets, he withdrew a piece of paper. Dialing a number, he waited. When the line was answered, he called, "Jace? It's Ryder Chase. Quick question. On your way out to Helberg, did any of you have tea?"

"Tea?" Jace stammered, "Yeah, from the farmer down the road. Pretty good stuff. Why?"

Chase hung up and stopped Wally as he was marching towards the van. The others looked on from the porch awaiting their next move. "The tea," Chase replied. "We need to check the tea!"

"I knew it was the farmer!" Jeffers looked elated, darting for the SUV. "Sohn, get on the phone for a warrant. Sheriff Biggs, have the hospital run a toxicology report on the latest vic."

Biggs nodded and dialed his phone.

When they arrived at the farmhouse, the stand was unmanned. Fewer than typical items lined the counter, though a big vessel of tea gleamed in the sun. Agent Jeffers looked anxious, peering around the farm for Stilton.

"Back again?" a voice called from inside the old barn. Farmer Stilton appeared, donned in his usual overalls and straw hat. He approached the group at the stand. "Vittles or official business?"

"Definitely business," Jeffers leveled at the man. "I need you to follow Agent Dunlap. You are under indictment for suspicion of serving tainted tea."

The farmer looked incredulous, "Tainted tea? What in tarnation are you talking about?" Stilton looked around at the crowd that had gathered, wondering if he was part of some elaborate joke.

"Sir, this is quite serious. We have a warrant to confiscate your tea and take it for laboratory analysis," Jeffers said evenly.

"Sheriff, this can't be for real," Stilton pleaded.

The Sheriff frowned, "I'm afraid it is Jamie."

Jeffers lofted the jug of tea while Dunlap escorted Stilton to the SUV. Putting him in the back, the junior agent slid into the driver's seat while Jeffers carried the tea. Agent Sohn stayed at the farm stand to collect additional evidence.

Within hours, the farm overran with forensics teams called in from Minneapolis. Every jar, canister, and Ziploc bag was had samples taken from them. An onsite laboratory truck pulled in front of the house, blocking the vegetable stand. One by one, specimens were brought in to be analyzed.

Agent Sohn ran a crew of agents blanketing the barn, every outbuilding, and the entire house. Labels were ignored. If it was a liquid, powder, or granule, it ran through diagnostics. Dr. Chase and his team stayed out of the way, watching the operation methodically comb through the entire farm.

"What do you think, Ryder…case solved?" Wally asked.

Dr. Chase looked thoughtful for a moment. Shaking his head, he responded, "No, not entirely. Even if there is some intoxicant found in Stilton's tea, it does not answer the consistency of reports from Helberg. It does not explain the connection to the house."

Tannen shrugged, "Implanted idea. The town knows about Helberg. The folklore is rich. Add in some sort of hallucinogen and bam, shared hysteria."

"Could be," Chase admitted. For a moment, the buzzing sound didn't resonate. There was such an energy from the team of agents combing the farm. It distracted him from realizing his phone was ringing.

Answering, received the initial report from the hospital via Special Agent Jeffers. The man they found that day had indeed been suffering from hypothermia. While he admitted the house was creepy, he didn't experience anything paranormal. Jeffers was delighted to point out that the man had not had tea either.

When Chase reported Jeffers' findings to his team, Wally rubbed his chin, "So, the man spent nearly the entire night in Helberg, without an incident."

"He admitted he never went in further than the foyer, and the storm outside superseded any sounds that would have been heard inside the house. By the time the storm abated, he had already succumbed unconscious," Chase shared.

"Guess you can't be scared to death if you're unconscious," Tannen declared.

"And perhaps not without some crazy laced tea," Wally added.

Agents Jeffers and Dunlap sat in the small Hope police station. Seated on either side of Stilton, they began their questioning. "So, what did you slip in the tea?"

"What are you talking about? Aside from honey, some citrus.... I made that berry one...you liked that one," Stilton pointed to Dunlap. "Nothing. I had other sweeteners and stuff for those who wanted to add it, but that's it."

"We have a dozen agents scouring your place right now. It will go easier on you if just tell us before we find it," Jeffers warned.

"I have nothing to hide. I wouldn't want any of those people hurt."

"But you have a beef with half the town. They shunned you. That had to make you mad," Jeffers pressed.

"Sure, but hurt people over it? They are still my neighbors; besides, you can't hide anything around here, why would I even try?"

"The perfect crime! Subvert through your tea, fuel the scares of the creepy old house on the edge of town. Even the way you planted your crops helped keep the legend alive," Jeffers boomed.

"I circumvented Helberg with my crops because I can't stand the place either. I sure the heck don't go poking in that old place," Stilton defended.

"Why, when the very idea mixed with whatever concoction you created did the job for you. You never had to step foot in the place," Jeffers said.

"I drank the tea, I had a reaction," Dunlap said. "This is very real, very sick."

"I am sorry for your troubles, but it was not my tea. That place, you shouldn't have gone in there."

Jeffers twisted his face, "Oh, stop it. The jig is up. There are no ghosts, just a hysteria-inducing mickey. My team will find it, and you will have no more room to bargain."

"I would help you if I could," Stilton pleaded. "I cannot tell you what isn't so."

"Your loss. Half a dozen deaths on your hands, you'll be locked up for a long time," Dunlap warned.

"Too bad North Dakota no longer has the death penalty. *Children* could have died!" Jeffers spat.

Stilton just stared at the two investigators. His eyes welled with tears. Jeffers' lack of expression belied his satisfaction. He had seen teary eyes from countless suspects when they realized they had been caught. It was rarely the act, but the finality of being busted that spawned that reaction. They had their man.

Breakfast the next morning was like déjà vu. The two teams sat around the breakfast table, planning their trip home and the closing of the case. Jeffers was beaming that the paranormal nonsense had been squashed by sound logic and a real criminal. All that was left to be done was determine which intoxicants had spiked the tea.

Agent Sohn brought the list from the mobile lab, and Jeffers was sifting through his emails to get the lab report on the confiscated tea. "Hmmm, report on the tea came up empty, but maybe he felt like we were closing in, and he stopped spiking it."

Looking at Danica Sohn, he asked, "What did the lab from the house come up with?"

Agent Sohn hesitated with her reply, "They, uh, they came up with nothing. There were no surprises in the chemical at the farm, from his kitchen or anywhere. They even tested every tea leaf."

"Then we missed it. It has to be around there somewhere," Jeffers demanded.

"The forensics team turned over everything at the farm. They even brought in dogs and ran the expanse of his fields – nothing," Sohn reported.

"Then he got rid of it," Jeffers stated flatly.

The group thought quietly about the situation. Agent Sohn finally spoke, "We have to let him go. The tea was just a theory. If a chemical or an ingredient was what caused those symptoms and those deaths, it is not at the farm now."

Jeffers let out a deep sigh. "It *has* to be!" Suddenly he snapped his fingers. "Helberg! Maybe that is the connection. He stashed his drugs at Helberg."

"Could be," Sohn nodded.

"Or we're wrong," Tannen replied evenly. "Maybe it's not the tea. It's something else. Maybe not even at the farm."

Jeffers did not like the idea of returning to square one.

Dr. Chase had been unusually quiet. Pulling on his lip, he took in the conversation. "Maybe I was wrong. After all, I drank the tea some of those nights with no reaction. Agent Sohn, you drank the tea and didn't have a reaction. The fire incident, did you have tea that day?"

"So, where does that leave us? Back to some freaking ghost again?" Jeffers snarled.

"Let's take your idea and search Helberg with the forensics team. Maybe they can find something that we missed," Dunlap suggested.

"Maybe they'll find a ghost," Wally grinned until his eyes crossed with the menacing pair belonging to Jeffers.

TWENTY-TWO

When they arrived at Helberg, the forensics team was already there, collection devices and equipment in hand. The generator attached to the top of the portable laboratory fired up and powering the analyzers inside.

Chase remained a bit despondent.

"What is it?" Wally asked his friend.

"I don't know. There is a weak but imperfect correlation to the tea. The farmer has his issues with the town, perhaps his eccentric behavior is part of some sociopathic psychosis, but I'm not sure I'm sold on that. I would think that as thorough a job as the team did, especially in the kitchen where the tea was prepared, a trace would have been picked up," Chase said to himself as much as in reply.

"Isn't it possible this place has some malevolent spirit that has found a way to exact revenge by burrowing into the central nervous system somehow?" Wally proposed.

"Anything is possible. Who says spirits don't evolve, just as mutated genes, they learn and experiment and find new ways of interaction," Chase shrugged.

"Maybe not a spirit, but the negative energy here has opened the door for a demon…" Tannen suggested.

Chase shivered. His teammates know as open as the professor was to ghostly beings; he had grave issues with any demonic. He wasn't sure what to believe in that realm, but he wouldn't touch a case that had such a reference. It was always his policy to defer.

"If that is so, it is out of our hands. Maybe that is why our techniques and our equipment failed to uncover anything. You still in touch with Fabian Da'more?" Chase asked Wally about the reputed demonologist.

"Yeah, I could reach out to him. Want me to fly him out?" Wally asked.

"Maybe. I don't believe the FBI team is going to find what they are looking for at Helberg."

"And I hope Da'more doesn't either," Tannen sighed.

Just as had happened at the farmhouse, the forensics team ripped through Helberg House. Floor by floor, room by room, every container, pile of dust, dripping liquid ran through analysis. Jeffers paced around, peering over the forensics team's shoulders like an expectant father.

He would follow a specimen into the lab and wait outside until the results had been processed. Snatching the reports, he and consulting with the pathologists, he would curse when they returned negative.

When the house itself failed to turn up anything of use, Jeffers instructed the team to scour the grounds. Again, any vessel that could hold a substance, any material organic or otherwise, was taken to the lab van to be analyzed. By dark, under the canopy of massive floodlights, the crew toiled. Desperation seized Jeffers' face. His mood soured severely.

When he got wind of the demonologist joining the investigation, he grabbed Chase by the collar and drug him to a darkened side of a forensics van. "Listen up, Chase. I appreciate your…help on this case. Your theory on the tea was a good one, but I am already looking like the horse's ass here. I have a dozen agents and pathologist working overtime with a state of the art lab trailer at an enormous expense to the taxpayers. We haven't turned up so much as a trace of anything hallucinogenic or potentially fatal laced into tea. The guy didn't even use conventional pesticides. I don't like having my career hinged on some paranormal lunacy. I have tolerated your team's antics as much as I can. Now you want some other nutball traipsing through here?"

"I don't like it either, to be completely honest. Every theory we have had has been tested and failed. We know people have died. We know the town's people, your people and mine have been afflicted. There is some evil here, human or otherwise. I don't know what other stones to turn over. There have been hundreds of cases purporting demonic influence. That is not my area. I stay away to the point I don't even have a real opinion as to its validity," Chase reasoned. "But, real or not, the reports do suggest in certain cases, the activity can be stopped."

Jeffers shook his head in disgust, "Do whatever you want. I need to send these people home before I am fired for wasting taxpayers' money." Storming off, the lead agent wrapped up the forensic team's search.

One by one, the trucks began to pull away. Jeffers marched around, giving orders, refusing to look the weary pathologist in the eye.

Agent Sohn found Chase fretting in a far corner of the property. "Demons, huh?"

"I don't know. Maybe…probably not. *Something* is going on here. I can't believe we have been wrong again," Chase said as the diesel engine of the lab truck roared to life and pulled away from the front of Helberg.

"The tea theory was a good one," Sohn shrugged. "Even if it wasn't the tea, if there was anything, we would have found it."

"And the farmer?"

"He was Jeffers' bet. He is refusing to let him go until the morning. Still holding out hope the evidence produces itself," the agent informed.

"I've never seen such an exhaustive search. Those guys were amazing. I think it is safe to say, the farmer is clean," Chase said.

"He did seem earnest. I mean, he's quirky and all, but a mass murderer? I'm not sure I ever bought it," Sohn shared.

The professor stared at the moon rising high above the cornfields. "I guess you never can tell what lurks inside of people. Throw in some heartbreak, desperation…who knows how they respond."

"True. We are taught that everyone can be a suspect. Still, we also learn a bit of intuition. His affect toward the town, irritated, but not angry. There's a difference," Agent Sohn reflected. "We FBI agents are experts in reading people, you know."

Chase stopped and looked at Sohn in mock incredulity, "And what do you read in me?"

Sohn smiled. Subconsciously, her tongue wet her lips, leaving them to glisten for a moment in the moonlight. "I see a man with great passion, a bit quirky, but brilliant just the same. A surprisingly deep man with a big heart and…"

Before she could on, one of Sheriff Biggs' officers came up to them with a small cooler in his hand. "It's been a long day. Sheriff sprung for cold drinks. Would you like a bottle of water or pop? There's different flavors."

"I could use a drink," Agent Sohn admitted. "I'll take a soda, any kind."

"I'll just have a water, thank you," Professor Chase accepted.

Snapping open their beverages, the two watched the officer walk away. They almost felt like school children who got caught passing notes to each other in class. Subconsciously, they created a little cushion of space between one another.

Listening to the officer pause at the next group of investigators, and share his spiel, a pair of words rattled in Chase's brain. Different. Flavors.

"Chase, what is it?" Sohn asked, seeing the change in the professor's expression.

"It's not the tea, well…not specifically. It's what's in one of the flavors of tea." He stood up and quickly made his way to Agent Jeffers, leaving Danica Sohn to trail behind him.

Sharing his thoughts with the lead agent, Chase was surprised when the anticipated reaction was not received. Instead, Jeffers just sighed and nodded. "Could be," was all the FBI agent could offer. Chase felt he understood. Too many failures, Jeffers was guarded by showing too much enthusiasm. He had already led the forensics team on multiple goose chases.

Still, the lead agent summoned one of the techs over. Then he stopped and looked at the professor. "Which flavor?"

Chase thought for a moment. His mind flashed through the team, the beverages they consumed, and their experiences. Agent Dunlap in the hallway bathroom, Wally with the late-night ghost army episode…they had both had the same flavor of tea. That would also explain why some had tea but no experience. Only some of the tea was at fault. Another related discovery danced in his head, but he was still grinding with it.

"Brambleberry. The farmer said it was the brambleberry."

Jeffers looked confused. "So, he had some berries added to the tea. Berries wouldn't cause that reaction."

"No…no they wouldn't. Unless…" Chase said thoughtfully. "Can I speak to Farmer Stilton."

Jeffers looked at the professor suspiciously, "I suppose. I'll call in." The lead agent tapped on his phone until he reached Sheriff Biggs and handed the phone over.

"Stilton, your brambleberry tea…what did you use in it?"

The farmer spoke back into the earpiece, "Blackberries, thimbleberries, a little sweet sage…why?"

"I think I have isolated the cases of victims with experiences to having ingested that flavor of tea."

After a pause, the farmer asked, "How would that cause the reaction?"

"I'm not sure," Chase admitted. "Are those ingredients indigenous to North Dakota?"

"Thimbleberries are from the west coast. I like them though. I grafted them to rootstock. The sage, that stuff is great. Adds a nice minty touch…. how is this helpful?"

Chase pulled at his lip. He was sure he was on the right track. He would hate it if he set Jeffers up for failure once more. "What rootstock did you use?"

"Wormwood. Nice, hearty, insect resistance. I try not to use pesticides on my land. Had to burn along the back half last season due to weeds, likely have to this year too, but no chemicals. Not on my farm!"

"Thank you, Mr. Stilton. This has been helpful." Chase handed the phone back to the FBI agent, who was looking on expectantly.

"Well...?"

"This might be it. He said he grafted the thimbleberries in the tea to wormwood. It's the main ingredient for absinthe. That was banned in the U.S. for nearly a century due to its psychoactive effects. It is a hallucinogen!" Chase replied.

Jeffers' face grew in excitement. "Nice work, professor."

Calling over his forensics lead, he explained what Chase had discovered. Together, with a growing contingent behind them, they marched behind the house to the farmer's berry patch. Locating the thimbleberries, the lead forensics agent kneeled on the ground and cut off a sample of the wood.

Wally, who had been looking on, pulled Chase aside as the forensics team, along with Jeffers, retreated to the lab trailer.

Chase sensed his tech specialist had concern, "What is it, Wally?"

"Wormwood. Nice idea, it's just the ban on it. The folklore, it was greatly exaggerated. The ban was lifted a few years ago. Chemists found the trace amounts of thujone-

the chemical they linked to addiction and effects on the CNS- were too small to have any appreciable impact on people. I doubt the grafting process, even shares any of the host plant's properties. Even if it did, it would be even more diminished," Wally explained.

"How do you know so much about wormwood?"

Wally grinned and shrugged, "I like absinthe. There is this great little bar that does the sugar drip…"

Chase sighed deeply. This revelation and the subsequent confirmation by the forensics lab would surely push Jeffers over the edge. He almost felt sorry for the FBI agent.

Wally beamed confidently, "I do think you are right about the brambleberry tea, though. I don't know how, but I have been reviewing all the times I drank it had an experience. It was when I drank the tea."

"Then, how? We have to figure it out before the lab results on the wormwood are complete," Chase declared, summoning Tannen over.

When the EMT came over, he asked, "What's up?"

Chase filled him on the situation.

"Yeah, Jeffers is going to blow a gasket. What do we do?" Tannen asked.

"The components have to be in the tea. We need to figure out how," Chase said.

"Alright. We have tea. The lab has analyzed that. It checked out," Tannen began running through the list.

"Ditto on the water," Wally chimed in.

"The berries, wormwood or not, will likely check out fine," Tannen added. "You said something about sage. Let's check it out." Tannen led the trio to the raised herb beds. Several species of sage flourished, nearly outgrowing the massive bed.

"Stilton can grow stuff, holy cow," Wally admired the abundant crop.

"He's got quite a few varieties. Some are medicinal. Let's see what we've got," Tannen searched on his phone to a plant identifier application. Finding the sage family, he walked the garden, stopping and noting each one the farmer had planted.

"He said the sage he used was minty?" Tannen asked. When Chase nodded, the Tannen held up his phone. "Could be this one. *Salvia divinorum.* Bingo. It says it has potent hallucinogenic properties. There is your army of ghosts parading down the street Wally."

"Could it cause the cardiologic effects?" the professor asked.

Tannen shook his head. "I don't think so. I mean, the delusion itself could, I suppose. But not in a healthy subject like Wally or Agent Dunlap."

Out of the corner of his eye, Chase watched Wally dodge and spin and flail away a honey bee. A wide grin crossed his face. "What weeds are around here?"

Tannen scrolled through his phone.

"Let's check the back edge of the farm," Chase suggested. Taking a direct path through the cornfield, they trooped across the property. The acreage, a rectangle running longitudinally, they enjoyed only have to manage the short side.

They didn't have to get to the end before they started noticing an invader into the cornfield. "Farmer Stilton said he had to burn along here last fall to wipe this stuff out." Chase pulled a sprig from the ground.

Wally took a picture of it and texted the image to a colleague at the university. A few moments later, he had a reply. He read it out loud, "*Sida corifolia*. Nasty stuff. Highly invasive, especially for wheat fields. Strong ephedrine-like psychostimulant affecting the central nervous system and the heart."

"Hallelujah!" Tannen cried.

Chase grinned, "Let's get back to the house!"

When they arrived back at the farmhouse, the forensics team was once again packing up. Agent Dunlap and Agent Sohn saw them and made a beeline for them. "Jeffers is on the warpath. He burst out of the lab cursing about the 'professor and his wild theories'," Agent Sohn warned them.

"I figured as much. Wally is apparently a wormwood aficionado and informed me I was wrong," Chase admitted.

Sohn wrinkled her nose, "What is that?"

"Half of a dangerous cocktail. We're sure of it this time," Chase stated.

"*Sida cordifolia*," Tannen announced. "A psychostimulant capable of inducing serious cardiac conditions, including a spike in heart rate and biothermal rates similar to ephedra."

Sohn looked suspicious, "And the other half? I thought you said the wormwood wouldn't do it?"

"It's not the wormwood. It is the minty sage Stilton used in his tea. The variety he used is called *salvia divinorum*, easily confused with *salvia officianlis*, or culinary sage. It adds a nice minty flavor but also a serious hallucinogenic effect!" Tannen beamed triumphantly.

"You guys are sure about this?"

Chase nodded.

"Alright, but…"

"Chase! You deluded, UFO chasing, hair-brained…you've likely cost me my job!" Jeffers bellowed as he approached the group.

"Yes, Wally informed me the wormwood wouldn't have the effect our victims had suffered," Chase admitted. "But, we have likely saved your job."

"And the people in this town," Agent Sohn added.

"Another theory? Please. How many have we run through? Each wasting my time and the entire pathology team," Jeffers fumed.

Chase thrust the weed in front of him, noticing the little fine hairs that shed from it to his hand.

"What is this?" the lead agent asked.

"Your answer, well, half of it, at least."

Jeffers studied the weed in his hand, "So the farmer put this...what is this... in the tea?"

"Well no. Not exactly..." Chase began.

Jeffers threw the plant on the ground and walked away in disgust.

The five remaining investigators watched the lead agent march off. Danica Sohn picked up the weed and dashed off towards the forensics trailer. The others followed.

"Agent Jeffers wanted this analyzed," she snapped as the pathology team was just battening down the mobile lab.

"And one more sample, Tannen?" Chase added nudging his tech towards the herb garden.

The pathologist shrugged and took the plant into the lab. When Tannen returned, he accepted the large sprig of sage as well.

The investigation party, minus Jeffers, paced out front.

"If this isn't it…" Sohn muttered.

"I know," Chase nodded.

"Maybe it is all paranormal. I mean, that is why you guys are here, right?" Agent Dunlap asked.

"Yes, but even so, I don't see how the events would cause the widespread cardiac and thermogenic symptoms without some neurologic agent," Tannen said.

At that moment, a voice cut into the group. "What the hell are you all hanging out for?"

"We uh, the lab…" Agent Sohn began.

Jeffers erupted, "You didn't give them that stupid weed? I didn't…"

The door to the trailer burst open, and the pathologist emerged with several papers balled in his hand, "It's just preliminary, but this looks promising, Agent Jeffers. We were starting to question your investigation…I'm not sure how you figured it out."

Jeffers stared at the forensics specialist, "The results?"

"Just as Agent Sohn said you had instructed. The combination of the sage and the weed, they create a powerful psychoactive stimulant, kind of like a very potent ecstasy," the lab director declared.

Jeffers shot Sohn a stern glare to which she returned a grinning shrug.

"So, the farmer, Stilton, he…" Jeffers began.

"Just as you thought, Agent Jeffers. Innocent," Chase cut into Jeffers further astonishment.

"The tea…" the lead agent tried desperately to piece it all together.

"Accidentally laced with a cross of the two components. Likely simply caused by the tiny hairs of the weed being carried through with bees as they did their natural pollination thing," Chase once more slipped in.

"Nice work, agent," the pathologist held the papers up in triumph and returned to his lab.

Jeffers stared at each member of the group. His eyes fell on his second in line agent.

"Dr. Chase and his team figured it out," Sohn stated.

"And you took it on yourself to have the lab chase down yet one more theory, in my name of all things."

"Yes, sir."

Jeffers stared thoughtfully. "I see. This is really over?"

Sohn nodded, "Long as the lab in Virginia backs up the results of the mobile, it would appear to be."

The lead agent turned his gaze to the paranormal team. "I guess I should thank you. Congratulations on a job well done. I am sorry I questioned your inclusion in this investigation. I'll be honest, I don't know how you pieced it together."

"Honestly, if Wally hadn't been so petrified of bees flying around the herb garden, I am not sure I would have. The berry-flavored tea had to be it. We couldn't give up when the rootstock was a dead end," Chase said.

"I'm glad you didn't," Jeffers admitted. "Turning to Sohn again, "You took a big risk putting that to the lab."

Agent Sohn looked at her superior directly, "I trust Dr. Chase and his team. Their theories may not always match ours, but their professionalism and passion for the truth does."

"Yes. Yes, I see that it does," Jeffers had to agree.

TWENTY-THREE

The scene in town was as if the investigation team had won the World Series, and they were returning to their home crowd. The people of Hope gathered to the steps of City Hall to show their appreciation. Ryder Chase sat for a moment and watched the people milling about in anticipation.

Then his eyes lighted on one woman in particular. He recognized her from the town meeting, the very first day they had arrived. She was the mother of Justin Marsh. Justin was the youngest victim to succumb to the cardiac symptoms and pass away. Through her smile, and relief for her neighbors and the rest of her family, Chase could see that her cheeks were stained with tears. Ryder understood. While they were successful, they were not in time for her son.

While Wally and Don Tannen exited the vehicle and relished the celebrity, Chase's mood remained even. When he got out of his seat, he offered a respectful wave and nod to the audience. Not stopping for questions, he headed straight for Mrs. Marsh.

When Chase was steps away, Mrs. Marsh offered a warm smile. "Thank you, and your team, Dr. Chase."

"I…," the professor began.

Mrs. Marsh stopped him, "I know. I wish you could have too." Scanning the rest of the town, most of which had gathered where they stood. "But you did for *them*."

Chase nodded, accepted her double handshake, clasping each other warmly for a moment. With a slight wink, Mrs. Marsh sent him back to the rest of the crowd, and she shrank away. Holding her youngest son's hand, she headed home.

For Mrs. Marsh, the scene was surreal as anything Chase had witnessed during the investigation. He watched as the federal agents tried to avoid the melee, and nearly did before Mayor Stenner of all people caught sight of them parking several blocks down the street from the hotel.

Chase chuckled as he watched the mayor and several others accost Jeffers and crew. Even from a distance, he could tell the Lead Special Agent was delivering his stock responses about not being able to answer any questions regarding an open investigation.

Suddenly arms and the scent of perfume enveloped him. Warm lips planted themselves on his before he could react. "Dr. Chase, you were amazing!" Abigail squealed.

Blushing, Chase backpedaled to a healthier distance. "I'm just glad we could help," the professor sputtered.

In the middle of the throng, he could hear Wally's voice elucidating on the perils of the investigation and how harrowing the Helberg was at night. Hearing his tech investigator suggest that he knew something non-paranormal was happening.

Wally and Tannen were busy signing autographs and sharing stories. Several women offered baskets of fresh baked goods, and one family brought a bag full of vegetables from their garden. Chase had nearly made it to the hotel when he felt a tug on his pant legs. He looked down and saw a little face flanked by pigtails staring up at him. Without a word, the little girl squeezed his leg and then wandered off to her mother.

Chase spun on his hotel room doorstep and faced the crowd. He watched as the mayor cajoled the FBI team down the street towards them. "You're a hero, Dr. Chase!"

"They are all heroes!" Mayor Stenner's voice boomed to a massive round of cheers.

When the voices calmed down, and then the entire investigation team had made their way to the hotel room doors, Chase addressed the crowd. "No. You are *all* heroes. What you endured here, with your friends and families. You had the courage to stand together as a community. You had the courage to ask for help with something there was no way you could explain, and if you did try to, you would be ridiculed. The way you support each other, the way you supported your storm-ravaged neighboring towns. You are an amazing people. We are blessed to have been able to serve you," with a wave, the professor disappeared into his room.

After a hot shower and a change of clothes, Ryder Chase flopped on his bed. His mind reeled, putting the events of the day and the week into place. Relieved that the town was out of danger and even the local farmer, though a bit eccentric, was not at fault. He had a nagging notion that not all of the mysteries had been solved.

The buzzing of his phone on the nightstand put a halt to his deep thinking and his rest. Jeffers called a wrap-up dinner meeting and even offered to allow the government to pick up the tab. Gathering his squad, he headed out for the diner.

As Chase stepped out onto the streets of Hope, the charming town seemed even more peaceful. All of the excitement and buzz had relinquished to hard-working families reconvening into their own lives. Approaching the diner, Wally and Tannen met him at his side. Through the diner windows, they could see the FBI trio had met before them.

Aside from one little older man sitting at the counter, finishing a slice of rhubarb pie, the investigation team had the diner to themselves. Agents Jeffers and Sohn sat opposite Agent Dunlap. Chase slid into the seat next to the junior agent while Wally and Tannen pulled a pair of chairs over.

Agent Sohn had a laptop in front of her, and Agent Jeffers leaned on a folder stuffed about three inches thick. Jeffers scanned the group for a moment. "I wasn't sure about having you guys on board. I don't think I was unclear about that. I was impressed with your dedication to science, and despite what you may have wanted to find on this investigation, you maintained discipline and remained objective. That is admirable."

The Special Agent in Charge addressed Tannen, "Your medical skills were top-notch and well used on this trip. Very impressive. The fact that you are a medic in the Reserves is quite apparent. You have been well-trained."

"Thank you, Agent Jeffers."

"Professor, excellent job piecing together the clues on the tea and the causative agents. Who knows how long it would have taken us to figure that out," Jeffers continued.

"If ever," Agent Dunlap chimed in.

"All that said, we have work to do to wrap this up. I wanted us to get the reports all done. We fly out of here tomorrow, we will debrief at Quantico the following day," Jeffers said and then looked at each of the paranormal investigators, "I have to ask, aren't you disappointed that the whole thing didn't turn out to not be ghosts?"

To a man, the team shook their heads. "No, not disappointed. Don't get me wrong, we love finding evidence, but above all, we like to find the truth," Chase replied.

"What is going to become of the farmer?" Tannen asked.

"He has already been released. He had no intention and no idea what his plants were doing. He certainly couldn't predict the combined effect the two plants would have. It's not like he's a real big fan on the weeds on his farm. The state Ag Board is going to come in and help with a procedure to get rid of those. As for his sage plants, the forensics team took the lot of them. He was happy for us to remove them," Jeffers reported.

Agent Sohn chimed in, "As you might imagine, he was mortified that it was his plants, his tea that was harming his neighbors. I think he is out of the tea business for good."

"That's too bad, he makes delicious tea," Wally groaned.

"You do remember that you could have died drinking that tea, right?" Tannen asked his friend.

Wally nodded, "Yeah, I'd choose the psychedelic, blood boiling, heart-stopping free version."

The group laughed wholeheartedly, trading barbs at each other for a few moments before Jeffers tapped at the file, "Alright. We're almost done. Let's get through this. It might take a while."

With their bellies full and their minds exhausted, Agent Sohn closed her laptop, and Agent Jeffers paid the bill with his agency Amex card. Thanking the diner owner for staying up for them, they headed back to the hotel for their last night in Hope, ND.

Agent Sohn and Ryder Chase held to the back of the pack as they sauntered their way across the street. "I like what you said to the town today," Sohn shared.

"This is a wonderful town. The people helped fight their own demon, and they won. Together."

"With a little help from the famous Dr. Chase and his team," Sohn added. "I saw Ms. Abigail got her parting shot in. Did she slip a note in your pocket for a last night rendezvous?"

"If she did, the dry cleaner is going to get a surprise," Chase quipped.

"Aw come on, she was kinda cute."

"Not half as cute as little Suzy Buchanan. She didn't even have to say a word, and she melted me," Chase admitted.

"Suzy who?"

"Suzy Buchanan was Mason's little sister. The teenage boy Tannen was able to save."

"Oh, she *is* adorable," Agent Sohn agreed.

"And then there is Mrs. Marsh. It is people like her that brings everything into perspective. She has lost so much. She holds herself very strong for the rest of her family," Chase said very sober.

"I can't say you guys are anything like I imagined...okay, maybe Wally is. You guys are surprisingly down to earth, very rational human beings," Sohn declared.

"Wow, that is quite the compliment. Why Agent Sohn, I find you to be a very rational human yourself."

Danica Sohn covered her face, "I'm sorry. That came out *way* wrong. It's just…listen. When we are no longer on the clock, maybe we could…"

"I would like that," Chase replied. His face hovered very close to hers. For a moment, they felt like they could finish what they started the night of the fair but they realized they were not exactly alone.

Closing her eyes, Danica Sohn simply nodded and backed away. In a much louder, more formal voice, she called, "Good night, Dr. Chase. It has been a pleasure to work with you."

"You as well, Agent Sohn," Chase replied, watching her and the other investigators retreat to their rooms. For just a moment, the professor considered following her and knocking on her door, but relented to retire to his own room, repeating to himself in a deep sigh, "You as well, *Danica* Sohn."

TWENTY-FOUR

By morning's light, in the aftermath of all that had transpired, the Helberg House loomed far less sinister. In the place of the dark shroud attached to the tales of haunts and the sadness of deaths, was an old piece of Americana. The old farmhouse stood in memory of a family and a little girl who had once been apart of the town, until tragedy afflicted them. The house in the wake of the tainted tea could now stand for a community that stood by one another and battled and survived.

"Not so scary now, is it?" Dunlap declared as all six investigators seemed to be taken in the final glimpses of the house.

"Just a sad old house," Wally agreed.

Dunlap looked thoughtful for a moment, "Say, Dr. Chase, the tea answered the victim's symptoms, but it doesn't answer the why the connection of Helberg."

The professor grinned as if relieved, someone finally asked the question. "No, it doesn't. We can theorize that from the deep folklore of the farmhouse, that it created a sort of group delusion when laced with the tea. Maybe the first incident got tied to Helberg, and that was enough of a seed to carry through anyone else who succumbed, including our crew," Chase paused for effect, "Or..."

"Or it is haunted!" Wally cut in grinning.

Dunlap looked wide-eyed, "Like the ghost took advantage of the toxicological effects of the tea!"

Jeffers grimaced, "I think I'm going to have to go with your first theory, professor."

Chase nodded and headed up the rickety, sagging porch. "Let's grab our gear and get going."

The process of pulling the cameras and recording equipment was a quick one with all six investigators pitching in. With only the basement left, Chase and Agent Dunlap volunteered to grab the last of it.

As the young agent plodded down the rickety steps after the paranormal investigator, he asked, "So, are all of your cases like this?"

"You mean involve an entire community, coroner's reports, and physical ailments....no," Chase replied.

"I kind of mean this exciting?"

Chase paused and looked at Dunlap. The glow of the flashlight pointed at the ground, offering just enough for visual contact. "It's probably like a stakeout for an FBI agent. Lots of waiting, listening, and watching for maybe one or two moments of relevance, if any at all."

"So, Helberg," Dunlap continued. "Not haunted?"

Chase shrugged. "The house was certainly not what was making people ill or killing them. We have lots of evidence we still need to go through. While we were finalizing the case at the farm, we kept our gear running, so who knows?"

"What about what we experienced here?" Dunlap pressed.

"So much of it was confounded with the tea reactions, it will be tough to sort out and label paranormal," Chase said.

Dunlap sighed, "Too bad. It would have been cool to walk away and say it was haunted."

Chase smiled, "Would've been."

The professor thought for a moment and then added, "Then again, I think this community might just benefit from having nothing lingering."

Dunlap nodded as he wound a cord around the last camera, "Yeah, you're right. They've sure been through a lot."

Giving one last glance around with the flashlight cutting through the dark basement, "I think we're done."

Stomping their way up the steps and to the foyer, it seemed almost sad to leave for Chase. He often had that feeling during an investigation. The buildings had so much history, so many stories to tell. He enjoyed them all.

Stepping out onto the porch, Chase followed Dunlap. Swinging the door shut, his eyes darted to Dunlap's. As the front door latched, a symphony of doors throughout the house slamming shut resounded in abrupt, successive booms. Frozen in place, their eyes acknowledged that each heard it. Listening intently, a crescendo of corn stalks clacking in the breeze rose all around them.

With an eyebrow lifted, Agent Dunlap queried, "Wind?"

Through a very unsure look, Chase nodded, "Yeah, wind."

Shaking their heads at the ever-contentious old house, they descended the steps and joined their teams at the vehicles. Stowing the remaining items they gathered from the basement, Chase nodded respectfully at the young agent as they retreated to their own vehicle.

Chase gave Helberg House one final look as he opened the passenger door. His glance forced him to do an immediate double-take. In the second-story window, the one reportedly belonging to Maggie, he swore he saw a little face in the corner of the lower right pane. As he looked again, the window was empty. Occasionally, a windswept cloud would brush by in its reflection. "Good luck to you, Maggie," he called softly.

Ryder Chase had barely begun to compile his notes on the investigation before he, along with his team, was seated alongside Special Agent Jeffers, Agent Danica Sohn, and Agent Dunlap. Chief Witt rubbed his eyebrows as he glanced over Sohn's report one final time before addressing the group.

Following a long pause, Witt studied the six investigators sitting before him. Looking pleased, he offered, "Not bad. From the report, it seemed you all had an integral role in reaching a satisfactory conclusion. Even managed to thwart a kidnapping and save a town ravaged by a tornado." Lifting the report, he looked disappointed, "What, no kittens in a tree to save to add to that?"

"We were merely advantageous to assist in ancillary service as were opportunistic," Jeffers responded.

"Well, it was good work. I have received letters of accommodation from the state Governor's Office, the mayors of Hope and Page, and a number of families throughout the region. I'm not easily impressed. I'm impressed," Chief Witt said, though his affect was as stoically stern as ever.

"So, at the end of the day, no crime committed. A freak happenstance of nature."

"Yessir, the state Ag Department confiscated all of the suspect plants for study and ultimately destruction," Jeffers confirmed.

"I see," Witt nodded slightly, "And the experiences at this...Helberg House."

"Officially unexplained," Chase piped in, "With the effects of the tea, the groupthink attributed to the lore of the house and the family's history and no clear evidence...a wonderful mystery."

Chief Witt grinned, "Trust me when I say, the FBI is pleased not to have to try and add haunting as a cause of death in a case file. And without you, Dr. Chase, perhaps the mystery surrounding the sudden deaths would still be ongoing."

"Dr. Chase was instrumental in piecing the connection with the tea, to the experiences, to the medical issues to the ingredients," Special Agent Jeffers confirmed.

"It sounds as though your two teams worked quite well together," Witt said.

Jeffers admitted, "I was resistant at first. Dr. Chase and his team proved themselves quite capable in numerous ways during our assignment."

"Excellent. I'm glad to hear that given I may have more work for you to combine forces on."

Jeffers choked, despite having grown amicable at the end of their investigation, he was in no way prepared to continue civilian involvement in future cases. "What?"

"It appears a town in Washington is overrun with reports of zombies," Witt said quickly, his voice losing some volume on the word "zombies".

Jeffers' face screwed into a painful expression, "Zombies, sir? You're joking."

"Given what you have been through, I think you are the perfect pairing to tackle this one."

"With all respect, Chief Witt, I've done my time with crazy paranormal stuff. How about Simpson and Crane? Those two new agents that just came out of the Academy?" Jeffers pleaded.

Witt shook his head, "You're on the docket. Dr. Chase, your team in?"

Ryder Chase looked at Wally and Tannen, both of who were grinning at him eagerly. "We're glad to help, Chief Witt."

Dunlap gave a celebratory fist pump in the air while Danica Sohn simply smiled.

Jeffers' sigh turned into a groan, "My career is over!"

Witt patted his senior agent on the shoulders, "I'm counting on you, Special Agent Jeffers." Landing a pile of dossiers in front of the lead agent, he smiled and began exiting the room. "You leave tomorrow."

TWENTY-FIVE

Sarah Whitman's heart was racing, pounding and clawing its way at her chest. Crouching behind a dumpster, she strained her ears. Erratic footsteps crunched along the gravel that covered the ground. She knew it was that gravel that alerted them to her presence in the first place.

She desperately scanned the area for her friends, but the tall, overgrown grass made it difficult to see anything from her crouched position. Her mind flashed to Eric, the last image of him made her stomach twist.

As they approached the old insane asylum, they thought they were going to have a good scare spooking each other in the old building. Long reputed for being one of the most haunted sites in the country, they never expected to find what they did. Even before they could step foot inside, the doors burst open and those things…Sarah grimaced at the scene etched in her memory…people…sort of.

Reaching the main entrance, they were surprised by a half dozen people. Snarling and spitting, they attacked Sarah and her five friends. Punching and clawing, they leaped on them. Sarah was able to wriggle away. When she looked over her shoulder, she saw Eric. On the bottom of at least three of them, they slashed and chewed on every portion of exposed skin. As she turned to run away from her pursuer, Eric was screaming, covered in blood, his flesh ripped apart.

Suddenly the footsteps stopped. She could hear her pursuer's wheezy breathing. In and out, it rasped. The sound sent chills down her spine. Sarah held her breath for fear it would alert her assailant to the dumpster. The crunching of footsteps resumed, heading back towards the entrance where Eric's screams finally stopped. Sarah feared she understood the reason why.

Collecting herself, she surveyed the fence line, trying to find the spot in the chain-link they had cut in to get to the asylum. They were surprised to find the property double fenced, much of it looking new. They assumed it was to keep trespassers like themselves out. Now maybe she understood it was to keep those…people in.

No longer hearing footsteps, she gathered herself. Taking in a large breath, Sarah launched herself in the direction of the tear in the fence. Her legs wobbled as she ran. Tears streamed down her face. Her focus narrowed to the thin cut in the massive wall of chain link. As fast as she could, she raced away from the awful place. She prayed she could be home with her family.

Behind her, she could footsteps heading in her direction. She didn't dare look back, instead remained focused on her goal. Every step seemed painfully slow. As much as she willed her legs to move faster, they maintained their gait. The footfalls came closer. She could hear heavy breathing. Step after step, she hurtled towards the fence through the tall overgrowth.

Somewhere in the grass and weeds, a fallen branch grabbed at her feet, snagging her shoe, sending her crashing to the ground. So close to her goal, the tears streamed down her face. Crawling in desperation, she clawed at the ground and kicked with her feet.

The footsteps behind her did not slow, and the imminence of them taking her over was clear. She didn't stop. Hand over hand, she crawled, slipping through the first layer of fencing. Nearly clear, hands clasped down on her ankle. In an instant, teeth clamped down on her, tearing at her heel, ripping flesh. Suddenly a scream erupted behind her, and a shadowy figure lunged beside her.

"Sarah, run!" her friend Michael, obviously already having breached the security fencing, saw her and came to her aid.

Pain searing through her ankle, Sarah pushed herself up, hobbling on her stable foot toward the outer fence. Michael kicked himself free and ran after her. Sarah had just slipped through the outer barrier, she turned to help Michael as a being leaped into the air and wrestled him to the ground. A second figure joined in rendering Michael helpless.

For the second time, her friend urged her, "Run, Sarah! Get out of here!"

With tears overtaking her cheeks, she hesitated for a moment. Realizing she had no choice, she complied. Dragging her left leg, she pushed herself away from the Northern State Asylum, relieved to be enveloped in the dark of night.

Made in the USA
Columbia, SC
15 January 2024

29549322R00181